Her Heart's Choice

A PRIDE AND PREJUDICE VARIATION

LEENIE BROWN

Leenie B Books
Halifax

Cover design by Leenie B Books. Images sourced from Deposit Photos and Period Images.

ISBNs: (ebook) 978-1-990607-31-8, (paperback) 978-1-990607-32-5, (large print) 978-1-990607-33-2

www.leeniebbooks.com

www.leeniebrown.com

Prologue

JANUARY 9, 1812

ALEXANDER MADOCH TOSSED THE newspaper he had been reading on the table and tapped the section he wished his friend Jonathan Lester to read. Then, he picked up a hunk of cheese, popped it into his mouth, and rising from his chair, walked to the window that overlooked the street.

Two horses, wearing the colours of his uncle's stable, carried a pair of finely dressed women toward the beach. The ladies were not alone, however, as a group of young swains followed close behind. He smiled as he watched the positioning of the gentlemen shift, one nudging the other out of the way to get closer to one or the other of the ladies.

"So the little termagant has decided to marry, has she?" Jonathan said, drawing Alex's attention back to the room. "I feel sorry for the chap that has to put up with her."

Alex turned from the window. "That chap shall be me. It seems we must make a trip to London."

"You? After the way she turned you out?" Jonathan shook his head and scowled. "I'd not be chasing after the likes of her again. Begone and good riddance, I would say."

Alex turned back to the window.

A young man was finally riding next to one of the young ladies. They were a good distance off, but still he could see how the young woman turned to the gentleman and slowed to allow him to ride more fully at her side.

He bit his lip and tilted his head as he watched the pair ride away. That was what he had wanted those many years ago: a lady, a particular lady, to ride away with him.

"She was not wrong in her refusal," he said without turning toward his friend.

Jonathan huffed his disagreement.

"The risk truly was too great. I had no guarantee of success." Alex glanced over his shoulder at his friend.

Jonathan pushed the paper away from where it lay in front of him. "You also had no guarantee of failure. As I see it, you had only to increase in your standing. Anyone admitted to your confidence knows how hard you work and how you do not begin a venture unless there is a very promising chance of success."

Alex remained looking out the window. It would do no good to argue the point with his friend, for he had whole-heartedly agreed with such a sentiment at first. In fact, if he allowed himself to consider it, he still felt somewhat bitter over the fact that Anne had not believed enough in his success to accept him.

"I did fall into some wonderful chances that I did not expect." He chuckled slightly as he turned toward his friend. "Would she not be surprised to learn of my connection to Prinny?"

When he had first arrived here, next to the sea, to take up his chosen profession, he had not expected that his uncle would be the one to help Prince George find his Brighton retreat, nor had he expected his uncle to recommend him for the position of manager of the Prince Regent's riding school and stables. His friend had also benefitted from the arrangement, because Alex had engaged him, as quickly as could be done, as his man of business and an assistant in his duties to His Majesty.

"That would put an end to her argument of your lack of connections," Jonathan agreed.

Alex began to nod his agreement but then changed it to a shake. "No." His head shook from side to side with more determination as his thoughts settled firmly into his mind. "No. Miss de Bourgh is not to know of my connections. None of them. Nothing beyond those I have through my uncle."

"Have you taken leave of your senses?" Jonathan's expression matched the disbelief in his words, and Alex could understand why. They both knew that convincing Miss Anne de Bourgh to accept anyone without a known title and fortune – or at the very least connections of the most excellent calibre – was going to be nigh unto impossible. Nigh unto impossible. Not entirely impossible.

Or so he hoped.

"I need her to accept me. Not my money and not my connections. I want her as my wife, but only if she accepts me without any..." His right hand circled in the air as if fluffing something. "... of those accoutrements."

Jonathan pulled the paper back to him. "Did you read this?" He lifted the paper and gave it a shake before scanning to find the announcement. "She has required that all potential suitors have, and I quote 'in their possession a title, as well as solvent and accurate financial reports,' and..." He held up a finger to emphasize his point. His tone dripped with disdain as he continued. "'Please be advised that references and documentation showing adherence to the above criteria will be required.' Exactly how do you propose to gain an audience with *her majesty* when you do not have a title and are unwilling to mention your connections?"

Alex chuckled to himself as he crossed the room and opened the door to call to the butler. Jonathan would not like this answer. Not even the tiniest bit.

Having given instructions to see that all was made ready for his trip, Alex turned, with a smile, to his friend. "How have I always gained an audience where none was extended?"

Jonathan groaned. "No. You cannot mean to make me assist you."

"It is your job."

His friend's eyes closed and after he had expelled a great sigh, he asked, "To whom am I to write about soirees?"

Ah, he knew he could count on Jonathan's cooperation even when he did not want to give it. They were too good of friends for something as monumental as pursuing England's most stubborn heiress and convincing her to capitulate her position to separate them.

"Do you still correspond with Brownlow?" he asked.

"On occasion, but that is a business matter and this..." he waved at the paper as he rose to follow his friend from the room.

"Is a business matter," Alex said to complete Jonathan's thought. "Your job is to see that I make all the proper connections and that all the required meetings are arranged so that I have the best chance of being successful in my enterprises, is it not?"

His friend sighed and shook his head. "Even though I still hold that this is not a matter of business, I shall give you every opportunity I can arrange. However, I will have you know that I am still not in favour of the idea."

That was easily seen – and understandable. A fellow could not have a better friend than Mr. Jonathan Lester. Alex clapped that staid and true friend on the shoulder. "As far as I am concerned, this is the most important undertaking in which you will ever take part. That is, of course, until you find yourself a lady of your own to pursue in earnest."

Jonathan groaned once again as they left the dining room.

Alex stopped abruptly and turned to face his friend. "We must not fail in this endeavour." He placed a hand on each of Jonathan's shoulders. "We simply cannot fail." A twice broken heart might not mend.

His friend nodded in an up-and-down, side-to-side sort of fashion that spoke of how difficult it was to say the words that accompanied the action. "Very well. I can see how important this is to you, and I will do my best to help you secure her. Though I question your sanity, I will do it for you."

"Thank you. That is all that I ask." A smile lit Alex's face. His happy future was just within his grasp – finally. "Now, to tell my uncle that I shall be leaving for town in two days."

As he exited the house, Alex expelled a great puff of breath as the burden of Anne's rejection those six years ago lifted, and his body and mind lightened. In truth, he had not felt such welcome vigour in some time. He had no doubt that the challenge that lay before him would tax him to the end of his patience. She always had. But... He drew a deep, satisfying breath as he walked toward the stables. The prize — ah, the prize for endurance would be satisfying indeed.

Finally, his heart would feel whole.

Chapter 1

JANUARY 21, 1812

As she hurried across the ballroom toward her cousin, Anne de Bourgh bit back a small smile at the expression of disapproval Mary, the new Lady Rycroft, gave him when he slid his arm around her waist and tugged her closer to his side.

Samuel – Lord Rycroft – had never been one to hold very firmly to propriety. Anne remembered him often getting into trouble for some sort of mischief every time he visited Rosings when he was young. Of course, he had not visited often, since her mother and his mother, though sisters, could only tolerate each other in small doses that were administered with years, not months, between them.

She sighed.

Her aunt, Lady Sophia, was easy to like. It was her mother, Lady Catherine, who was the challenge.

Not even Anne could tolerate her mother's constant nattering and interference for any length of time. It was why she had feigned illness so often and had hidden in her room. She could not hold back her smile this time. On how many of those occasions had she escaped from her mother by taking to her room and climbing down the trellis? The number was not small!

"You are even more beautiful when you smile." Mr. Blackmoore, the living, breathing annoyance whom Anne had been attempting to avoid all evening, stepped into her path.

Her lips ceased smiling and instead curled as they did when she was forced to take that dreadful concoction her mother had gotten from the apothecary and insisted on giving to her at the first sign of a sniffle. No! That was unfair to the concoction. This gentleman left a far less pleasant taste in one's figurative mouth simply by being. Why could he not understand her refusals? She made no reply as she attempted to step around him.

"Come, Miss de Bourgh," he said, taking her by the elbow, "a dance is about to begin. Will you not join me?"

Anne pulled her arm away from him. "Indeed, I will not. I have told you more than once that I do not wish to make or keep your acquaintance." Again, she endeavoured to step around him only to be prevented.

"Miss de Bourgh, it is just one dance. How can you deny me the pleasure of such lovely company as yourself? Surely, you cannot be so cruel."

Anne crossed her arms and chuckled mirthlessly. "I assure you that I can be." She was her mother's daughter after all, which meant she could be rather immovable, and unpleasantly so, when she chose to be.

"Blackmoore." Lord Rycroft's voice held a warning. The gentlemen, though friends, had not re-established the camaraderie they had shared prior to an incident involving Mary.

"Rycroft." Mr. Blackmoore nodded his head in greeting.

"I did not invite you to this soiree to harass my guests." Rycroft tipped his head to the side and raised a brow. Anne could see the slight clenching of his jaw and knew that he was more than just a little disturbed by the actions of his former friend.

"I was merely asking Miss de Bourgh for a dance."

Rycroft shifted his gaze to Anne. "And does the lady wish for a dance?"

"If she does not, then she shall have to sit out the entire evening." Blackmoore smiled at Anne. It was not a friendly smile but one of cunning and calculation, and exactly the type of smile that Anne despised the most.

"My card is full," she lied.

"Surely not." Blackmoore's hand reached out to take her card, but Anne quickly pulled her hand out of his reach.

"This is not my card, sir. I fear I have left my card in the retiring room. I was just on my way to ask if Lady Rycroft would accompany me to retrieve it."

"Not your card?" Blackmoore's tone spoke of disbelief.

"That is what I said." Anne smiled as her eyes held firmly to his for a moment before she dipped a curtsey and, with an *if you will excuse me*, stepped around Blackmoore and hurried toward Mary, leaving her pursuer to her cousin's care.

She stamped her slippered foot and crossed her arms as she came to stand next to Lady Rycroft. Her mother would be horrified because a lady did not stamp her foot. However, at the moment, as Anne scowled at Mr. Blackmoore, she did not care what a lady did or did not do.

"He is without equal," she muttered with her eyes still on Blackmoore.

"Are you well?" Mary asked.

Anne turned her attention to Mary. "I am well, but he is not. There is something seriously wrong with that man's head." Her hand flew to cover her mouth as she realized that Mary was not alone. "Forgive me." Her cheeks flushed crimson. "I struggle to keep my thoughts to myself at times."

Lord Brownlow chuckled. "That is a trait that is not unlike your cousin."

"Indeed," Mary said with a laugh and a gently pointed look that made Anne wish she had cared a trifle more about what a lady did or did not do before she had acted and spoken so freely.

"Lord Brownlow," Mary continued, "this is Miss de Bourgh. Miss de Bourgh, Lord Brownlow."

"A pleasure," Brownlow said with a bow.

"Is it?" Anne said in surprise.

Again, Lord Brownlow chuckled. "It is."

"Then, I thank you," she said with a curtsey before turning to Mary. "I fear my determination to avoid a certain situation requires me to ask you to accompany me to the retiring room." She glanced back toward where Blackmoore and Rycroft still stood conversing.

"As much as I would like to continue talking to Lord Brownlow," she smiled at the gentleman, "I find that doing so puts me at risk of speaking to *him* again," she tipped her head toward Blackmoore, "and I have no desire to do so."

"If you are positive it cannot wait –"

"It cannot. I assure you." The faster she was away from that man, the better.

"Well, then, I shall accompany you. Lord Brownlow, if you will excuse us."

"Certainly, Lady Rycroft, Miss de Bourgh." He nodded to each lady in turn.

Anne began to walk away from him but then stopped and returned. "Do you have a dance that is free?" she asked in a whisper.

"I do," he whispered in reply.

Anne cast a wary eye toward Blackmoore. "Which one?"

"The one after supper remains open."

"That will do," Anne said. "I look forward to dancing with you, and I do apologize for being so forward, sir. However, I may have told *someone* that my card was full, and I must now fill it."

Brownlow chuckled softly. "If you need a second dance, Miss de Bourgh. I have the last of the evening available as well."

Anne sighed, and her shoulders drooped in relief. "That would be most helpful."

"I am pleased to be of assistance." Lord Brownlow shook his head as she scooted away.

Mary took Anne's arm as they left the ballroom. "You do know that ladies are not to ask gentlemen for dances, do you not?"

Anne nodded. "I would not have done so if it had not been necessary." She looked up and down the hall, and, seeing that no one was near and feeling confident that she would not be heard, she continued. "Mr. Blackmoore insists on importuning me at every turn. I could not see a way to avoid dancing with him and still be allowed to dance with others." She smiled sheepishly. "So, I lied." She looked away from the disapproving look that Mary gave her. "I know it is wrong," she said softly, "but I should be able to refuse a man like him without refusing all others."

Mary patted Anne's hand. "I agree that it is not fair."

"If you would rather…" Anne looked up at Mary, who, like Kitty and Elizabeth, had become a dear friend over the past two weeks. "I could plead a headache and borrow a room in which to rest."

Mary shook her head. "There is no need for that. We shall just have to find enough gentlemen to fill your card so that your words no longer remain untrue."

And so, they did. With Mary's help, Anne's card was full before they had returned to the ballroom.

For much of what remained of the first half of the evening, Anne remained near Mary or Lady Sophia, which had been quite the delightful and revealing experience, for she had not realized just how pleasant it could be to sit or stand near someone who did not constantly remind you to straighten your posture or smile more engagingly or less widely or less frequently or more often.

And she had even managed to sit for supper without her mother near! It may not have been a miracle above all miracles, but to Anne it was no small thing. When the meal was over and all exhibitions of talent were completed, Anne once again sought to limit the amount of time she had to spend with her mother.

After one particularly lively dance in the latter half of the evening, Anne, at Lady Sophia's insistence, took a seat not far from an open balcony door. The breeze was refreshing, and Anne closed her eyes and filled her lungs with the deliciously cool air.

Her feet were beginning to hurt, and she was certain her arms would be nearly unusable by morning. She had not realized just how much exertion there was in dancing. It was tiring, but the fatigue was not unwelcome. In fact, she found it exhilarating. She had not enjoyed herself this much since the last time she had sneaked out of her bedroom to ride. Riding had always been a pleasure to Anne, but her mother disapproved of too much exertion and exposure to the elements.

Anne was just beginning to ruminate on the ridiculousness of being confined to one's room to preserve one's health when she heard a familiar and unwelcome name.

"Madoch," Lord Brownlow said, "I feared you were not going to show."

"I do apologize for my tardiness, but I had an unexpected call to which I had to attend. There really was no avoiding it."

Anne cautiously turned to look at the speaker. It could not be *him*. It simply could not be. *He* was not of the gentleman class. She paused and sighed. Perhaps she was lowering him a bit more than he deserved. His father was a gentleman, but he was a second son, that much was true.

Her breath caught in her chest as her eyes found the gentleman standing with Lord Brownlow. "Alex," the name fell from her lips on a sharp exhale. It was him! He was here. How could he be here? Why was he here? Did he not still reside in Brighton? Why was he in town?

Oh, this was not good! He could not see her. He must not see her. Her heart might break a second time if she had to actually speak to him. She glanced from him to the open balcony door and then back to him, before rising from her seat and making her escape.

Chapter 2

THE AIR OUTSIDE THE ballroom was even cooler than the breeze Anne had felt inside, for, out here, there were no throngs of dancing people nor were there scores of candles casting their light and warmth. There were a few torches and lanterns, but not enough to do more than scatter the shadows of the night.

She folded her arms and rubbed the upper parts of them as she looked left and then right. If she remembered correctly, the library was to the right, three windows down, and open. That is the door to the garden had been open when she and Mary had gone looking for her cousins, Darcy and Richard, to fill her dance card. She certainly hoped no one had closed it, for she knew that being both alone and so far away from her chaperone was putting herself at risk, but what was she to do? *He* was in the ballroom, which meant she could not be.

Everything would be as it should be just as soon as she reached the safety of the library. Kitty and Richard had not been seen for a while. So, it stood to reason that Kitty had probably required a rest again since her head was still not quite right after her fall and required her to frequently seek solitude.

Therefore, even if the door was closed, they would let her in, and then, everything would, indeed, be well. With that in mind, Anne began heading for the library as quickly as could be done without looking like a fox fleeing a pack of hounds.

As she went, Anne considered how feigning a head injury might be a handy way to avoid her mother. It was an option she had not yet attempted to this point in her life. It could work, and for an extended amount of time. But then, would the care required to attend to such an injury be too much to bear?

She stopped to consider the option. No, it would not do. Her mother would hover or have a surgeon posted outside her door. That was most certainly not the wished-for result. Chances and new schemes were often worth the attempt but only if they did not lead to her avoiding one untenable situation merely to be cast into another that was far worse. One must always – or most times, at least – consider carefully the ramifications of what one pretended.

Of course, there were moments when there just was not time to ponder every eventuality – such as when a lady's uncle and mother were arranging an unwanted marriage for her or when a lady needed to make a quick exit to avoid a former suitor who still caused her heart to ache whenever she passed a stable of horses.

Still quite lost in her thoughts, she began slowly walking toward the library.

The stables at Rosings had not been nearly as pleasant an escape in the past six years as they had been before the day when she had sent Alex away. It had been the right decision. She knew it was, but that did not make it any less painful – not then, not now.

Footfalls on the stone of the balcony broke into her thoughts, and after giving a glance over her shoulder, she lifted her skirt and made to run the few remaining steps to the library.

However, Mr. Blackmoore was quicker than she and had her by the arm before she could flee.

"Miss de Bourgh, it seems we are meant to marry."

"Marry?" Her heart climbed into her throat as the reality of the situation in which she found herself settled into her startled mind. She twisted and pulled at the arm he held. "I think not!" She could not marry him.

He slid an arm around her and hauled her closer to him. "But we are in a very compromising position, are we not?" He wore that sly smile of his once again. "Such a scandal as this will put to an end any other offers of marriage but mine." He bent his head to kiss her, but she turned her head to the side and pushed at his chest.

"I would rather die an old maid than be married to the devil." She turned her head the opposite direction of his mouth once again and pushed some more.

He chuckled near her ear. "The devil?"

The feeling of his breath on her skin made her shiver in revulsion. She pushed against him again. "Yes, the devil. Who else traps a lady into marriage just so he can keep his mistress and his money?"

"You would be surprised to know how many do just that." His mouth was still near her ear, and he whispered into it before kissing it.

Anne gasped and without thought slapped him. "Libertines, the whole lot of them," she cried. "Unhand me at once," she demanded as she continued to struggle to get away.

"No, not until you have consented to marry me," he growled as his grip on her twisting form tightened.

"I cannot. I will not. I would rather –"

"Darling, I have found your dance card." The voice that broke into Anne's protest was not only a familiar one but also the very one which she had been attempting to avoid by coming out here. Relief at being saved warred with her wish to flee from both him and Mr. Blackmoore.

"It was rather foolish of you to hold it so loosely as to let it fall into the border," Alex continued as he joined her on the balcony.

Mr. Blackmoore's arms fell away from Anne, and she spun from him and nearly straight into her rescuer.

"Thank you, Mr. Madoch." With a trembling hand and a curious look, she took a dance card from him. Whose card it was she did not know.

He smiled at her just as he had always smiled at her. It was an open, unaffected smile, a smile of true delight.

Her lower lip trembled, and she sucked it in between her teeth. No one else in her life had ever smiled at her like he did. It was one of the things that had made it so hard for her to turn him away the last time they had met.

"It took a bit of searching." His voice was calm and reassuring. Oh, if only he was not a second son! "And I fear my shoes may be too soiled to enter the ballroom again, but there it is. A prize by which to remember this night."

She nodded her head in place of saying *thank you*, since speaking would put her in danger of crumbling into a weeping mound of tattered pieces.

He took one of her hands and spoke in a low voice. "Perhaps a few moments in the library would be beneficial. I saw one of your cousins at the window."

Again, she nodded as she clutched desperately at her unruly heart while the way he had always been so kind to her flooded her memory. His small touches. His companionable silence when she did not wish to speak because of some tumult of emotions. His ability to think ahead and avoid any further harm befalling her, even if it meant putting himself at risk.

"I will just make sure that this gentleman has made it back to the ballroom before I join you." His voice rose slightly in question, making his tone match the look in his eyes.

She pulled in a silent breath. "Of course," she managed to say without so much as a tear finding its way to her eye.

Truthfully, she did not wish to see him in the library, or anywhere, for that matter, but he had just rendered her a great service and the alternative of being left here with Mr. Blackmoore was, without a doubt, the worse choice. So, she gathered her thoughts and her strength and walked as calmly toward the library door as she could.

When she reached it, she looked back. Alex stood in front of Mr. Blackmoore with his arms crossed. He was shorter than Mr. Blackmoore by at least three inches, and his build was slight as far as gentlemen's figures were judged. However, she knew from watching him work with the horses in the paddock at Rosings that his size belied his strength.

She could hear Alex's rumbling angry tone. It wasn't just his strength that was great. His courage had always seemed to be unconquerable to her. She shook her head. He had always stood as her protector. Her heart sighed while a tear formed in her eye and she blinked it away. If only he had the means and position to meet her qualifications, her search for a husband would be over.

"But he does not," she whispered sadly to herself as she stepped into the library.

Chapter 3

"Anne?" Richard, who was standing near the library door that opened to the garden, caught her by the arm to prevent her from stumbling as she stepped into the room and directly into him. "What brings you to the library by way of the balcony?" His surprise was mingled with suspicion, and he did not release her arm though she had kept to her feet. Instead, he guided her to where Kitty was sitting. "And without a wrap?" There was censure in the question. "You are positively frozen!"

Anne dutifully took a seat next to Kitty. She knew that when her cousin started using the tone he had just used, there was very little chance of doing otherwise. As sweet and gentle as he could be, there were times, such as now, when he towered over her and spoke with such an air of authority that she knew for certain he was indeed Lord Matlock's son.

"I needed some air," she muttered. "I know it was foolish to go out without my chaperone, but…" Her voice trailed off as she saw him fold his arms and shake his head.

"You were outside in the dark, alone?"

She lifted her chin. "I was. At first. But then, Mr. Blackmoore discovered me, and he would not unhand me until

Mr. Madoch appeared." Anne huffed. "The rules of society and propriety are insufferable." She folded her arms and glared back at her cousin, bracing herself for whatever battle she might be starting. She was not in any frame of mind to be scolded by him. What she had just endured was punishment enough for her foolishness.

To her surprise, he shrugged. "They are." He took a seat near the settee where Anne and Kitty were sitting. "Be that as it may, it is not advisable to ignore those rules unless you are prepared to pay the price." He took Kitty's hand which was nearest to him in his own. "And the price can be very high indeed."

"So it can be," Darcy said as he joined them. "Although…" He pulled his wife close to his side. "There are times when doing so has produced a most pleasant result."

Anne rolled her eyes. Her cousin spoke, of course, of his being required to marry his wife – with whom he was utterly besotted – because of a supposed indiscretion.

"Mr. Blackmoore is not a pleasant result." She shuddered at the thought of being forced to marry *that* ne'er-do-well.

"And that is why we must follow the rules as closely as we can." The comment might have been a scold if it had been spoken by anyone other than Kitty. Her soon-to-be cousin's voice was soft and reassuring, as if she were merely agreeing with Anne. If she spent all her life searching, Anne was certain she could never find another lady so sweet as Kitty to be her friend and relation.

Just as Anne was giving Kitty's hand an appreciative squeeze, the door, through which Anne had only moments ago entered, opened.

Alex closed the door as quickly as he could but still, it was not fast enough to keep a cool breeze from following him into the room. His eyes scanned the gathered group. He had known that at least one of Anne's cousins was in the library, but he had not expected to see quite so many people. He stood for a moment not knowing exactly what he should say to so many people, all of whom were looking at him in surprise.

Finally, he stepped forward and bowed. "Alexander Madoch." An introduction was usually the best way to start in any situation when one was presenting himself.

"Madoch? Not the same Madoch that used to skulk around Rosings' stables and plague the stable master with questions and suggestions?"

It would be Anne's cousin Darcy who would remember him. How many times had they met in the stables? Darcy was forever escaping the confines of Rosings when he was visiting. From what he understood, Darcy had never gotten on well with Lady Catherine – likely because the lady insisted on him marrying her daughter whether either of the pair wished it or not.

Such a trying household Anne had grown up in! It was quite a deal worse than his own, and yet, he and his father had had their share of disagreements.

Alex bowed his head in acknowledgement of Darcy's statement. "One and the same."

"I have not seen you in years." Darcy stuck his hand out in welcome. "How have you been keeping yourself?"

"He has been working for his uncle in Brighton," Anne supplied as Alex shook Darcy's proffered hand. "Or so I have heard," she added softly when all eyes, including his, turned in her direction.

"Miss de Bourgh is correct. I joined my uncle in Brighton five, or was it six, years ago?" As if he did not know how long it had been since the day when she had refused him.

"Six years ago, November." She pressed her lips together as if she had not meant to answer.

He smiled at her. It was good to know she had not forgotten him.

"I believe you have the right of it. It was six years this past November." He turned his attention back to Darcy. "My uncle owns a stable in Brighton. It is a popular establishment with those who come to visit."

He glanced at Kitty and then Elizabeth. "I am fairly certain I know you two gentlemen as Mr. Darcy and Colonel Fitzwilliam, but I am at a loss as to who these lovely ladies are."

"Forgive me," Darcy said. "This is Mrs. Darcy, and seated next to Anne is Mrs. Darcy's sister, Miss Bennet."

"Soon to be Mrs. Fitzwilliam." Richard smiled proudly. "And I am no longer a colonel but happily a mere mister."

"Congratulations to you both." Alex had, of course, heard from Lord Brownlow, at whose house he and Mr. Lester were staying, the full story of each of the gentlemen's now happy circumstances.

"What brings you to town?" Richard asked.

"Business," he said with a glance toward Anne. She would be most displeased if he were to mention just what sort of business he had in mind, and the thought nearly stopped him from revealing it — nearly. However, he was not one to back down from a challenge. "I am, in fact, here to marry Miss de Bourgh."

Anne's eyes grew wide, and she gasped. "You cannot."

"Oh," he said with a smile, "I think I can." And he was determined to succeed.

"But you are not titled or wealthy," she protested.

He shrugged. "Yes, well, that is what we shall have to discuss at our meeting tomorrow when I call on you."

Anne rose to her feet. Panic filled her eyes. "You are not to call on me. I will not be home to you."

"Not home to a friend? How very odd and rather improper."

Her eyes narrowed as her arms folded in front of her.

Alex turned back to the two gentlemen who were both looking at him with concern. "I assure you, gentlemen, that my intentions are entirely honourable. In fact, it is not the first time I have sought to marry Miss de Bourgh, but she was not ready to..." He glanced at Anne. "How did you put it? Oh, yes, she was not ready to sign her life away at that time." He grimaced slightly at the memory of her cutting remarks about his being wholly unsuitable due to his lack of connections, lack of wealth, and plans for his future.

"However," he continued, "according to the paper, she is now ready, and so, I am here to present my suit."

"You have read her requirements, have you not?" There was a tone to Darcy's voice that spoke to his concern for Madoch's mental faculties.

"Oh, I have. More than once," Alex assured him. "Miss de Bourgh is correct when she says I do not meet all of them." He chose his words carefully so as not to be false but also so that they would not reveal his true standing. If she were to choose him, he was determined it would not be for his wealth or position. "I think you gentlemen would agree that there are more important things than a title and money to consider when choosing a marriage partner."

Anne huffed. "Well, of course, whomever I choose must be pleasant and of good moral character." Again, she pressed her lips together as if she had not meant to speak.

Alex tipped his head to the side and stared at her for a moment, taking the time to learn the little changes that had occurred to her features due to the passage of time. It had not changed her beauty. If anything, it had added to it. Hers was a face he could watch for hours.

"That is true," he said at last, "but I spoke of the heart." He continued to look at her as she bit her lip and schooled her face not to reveal the emotions that shone in her eyes.

"One must not be ruled by one's heart," Anne said softly.

He nodded. "That is where you have always been wrong."

Though the comment was spoken so softly that it was barely heard, he was certain from the silence which followed it that the message of his words was not lost on Anne or the others watching the exchange. His heart lay open before them all, and he knew it. But one did not win what he wanted by avoiding daring attacks. Not that such stratagems were easily done.

He drew a breath and released it. "I have stayed long enough. I just wished to assure myself that Miss de Bourgh was well and had not suffered any ill effects from her encounter with Mr. Blackmoore."

"I am well. Thank you."

He studied her face a moment longer. "I am happy to hear it. Until tomorrow," he added with a bow.

"I will not be home," she called after him.

"Then, I will wait for your return."

He smiled as he heard her huff and stamp her foot. He had always loved her indomitable spirit.

"My lady," he said with a bow as he held the door open for Lady Sophia. Then, with one last look at Anne, he made his way toward the ballroom to let Brownlow know he was leaving.

Chapter 4

LADY SOPHIA SAT DOWN next to Anne. "Where have you been?" She wrapped her arms around Anne's shoulders and drew her close. "I have been so worried about you." She pulled back a bit so that she could look at Anne's face. "Do you know how hard it is to keep a step ahead of your mother? Imagine if she had asked me where you were, and I did not know." She pulled Anne close again.

"I should be furious," she said gently as Anne apologized. "Now, tell me what it was that made you seek an escape."

"Mr. Madoch," Anne whispered.

"Mr. Madoch?" She looked from Anne to Darcy and then Richard, who both nodded. "Do I know him?"

"Perhaps," Darcy answered. "He used to spend a good deal of time in Rosings' stables."

Lady Sophia shook her head. "I have not visited Rosings that often, and even if I had, that still does not tell me why my niece disappeared from the ballroom without a word to me or anyone else."

"He is a former friend from years gone by," Anne supplied when her aunt gave her a questioning look. "I saw him and did not wish to speak with him, so I decided to come to the library."

Lady Sophia held up a finger to keep Anne from saying anything else. "Just like that? You left one room and ended up in another without any trouble on the way?"

"That was Madoch who was just leaving as you entered," Richard inserted.

This comment caused Anne's favourite aunt to scowl the tiniest bit and look at her for an explanation. So, after drawing a fortifying breath, she shared her tale about how Mr. Blackmoore had stopped her to press his suit in a most ungentlemanly way until Mr. Madoch had come to her rescue.

"Well, that was quite an adventure." She sighed. "You do realize, do you not, that you may have put yourself in a very precarious position." She glanced at Darcy and Richard. "If Mr. Blackmoore were to make it known that he was in the garden with you…"

Anne's eyes grew wide, and she shook her head. No, no, no! It could not come to that!

Lady Sophia shrugged. "Gossip has power."

Anne's heart hammered a fast rhythm in her chest, and the unpleasant fluttering that the thought of being Mrs. Blackmoore brought to Anne's mind made it impossible for her to remain seated. She paced to the window and back. "I will not marry that man." She turned to her cousins. "He has a mistress, you know."

They both nodded.

"What else can be done?" Lady Sophia asked softly. "A lady's reputation is a fragile thing, and once damaged, it is nearly impossible to restore. However, I suppose we are worrying before it is needed, and I believe you are engaged for the last set of the night, so we should make sure you are there to fulfill your obligation and to be seen." She stood and held her hand out to Anne.

Anne dutifully allowed her aunt to return her to the ballroom, though she had no desire to go there. She was not in a mood to dance. She was not in a mood to be pleasant. She wished to find a corner in an empty room and have a good cry — first, for her stupidity in sneaking out, and then, for the broken bits of her heart, which she had thought were healed until she had seen *him*.

She sighed as she took her place across from Lord Brownlow. If only Alex had not shown himself, she could have married for advantage without the renewal of the pain of sending him away, for she knew that she was going to have to send him away again and that it would be no less painful now than it had been six years ago.

There was no way she could marry him. He was not titled, nor did he have wealth, and without those things, she simply would not marry any man, including him. Her heart's resolve faltered for a moment, and for a few steps of the dance, she considered that perhaps a title was not necessary, as long as there was money enough.

She smiled and replied to the question Lord Brownlow asked, and then, slipped back into her thoughts.

No, a title, indicating a position that made it difficult for others to bend your will to theirs, was an absolute necessity. She had seen the truth of it. It was a non-negotiable requirement, and Alex had neither wealth nor position. Therefore, he was an unacceptable choice, no matter how much her heart might protest the fact. With that decided, she turned her attention more fully to the dance and her partner.

As the dance ended and Anne curtseyed to Lord Brownlow, a lady to her right bumped into her lightly.

"I beg your pardon," the lady said.

Anne nodded her acceptance of the apology and was about to move on when the woman spoke once again. "You are Miss de Bourgh, are you not?"

"I am."

"I am Miss Ivison."

The lady would have taken Anne's arm after introducing herself if Anne had not pulled it away. Such forwardness was never acceptable in Anne's opinion.

"I have heard of you," Miss Ivison continued, stepping close to Anne. "You put an advertisement in the paper for a husband, did you not?" She smiled coyly before looking toward the door as if trying to locate someone. "I wonder how cool it will be in the carriage on the way home. Did you find it cold in the garden? Or did Mr. Blackmoore keep you warm enough?" With a triumphant look, she curtseyed and made to move away, but Anne's hand on her arm stayed her.

"Where have you heard such tall tales? Me? In the garden? With Mr. Blackmoore? Indeed!" She shook her head and chuckled as if the idea were completely preposterous.

Miss Ivison picked Anne's hand up off her arm and let it drop as if she were removing a piece of lint. "I have had the story from Mr. Blackmoore himself." She gave Anne an appraising look. "At least his tastes are better than I had thought. I had heard it rumored that he was considering Miss Bingley." She made a sound of pitying regret before adding. "Caroline is invaluable to me for her connections to soirees such as this, but do consider it. A man of rank marrying a lady from trade?" She chuckled. "Congratulations for preventing such a travesty." Her left eyebrow flicked up, and her lips curled into a smug smile before she left Anne.

Anne was sure her heart had stopped. She stood in shock for a moment and watched Miss Ivison walk away; however, shock did not take long to turn to anger and anger leapt very rapidly to fury as her eyes searched the room for her prey.

Finding whom she sought, she began to cross the room. People were bidding each other good night and filtering out the various doors to the ballroom as she reached her quarry. She stood for a moment behind him, listening to the tale he was telling.

"She was quite willing," he whispered, "had the night not been so cool..."

The gentleman to his left cleared his throat just as Anne tapped Mr. Blackmoore on the shoulder. His eyes grew wide as he turned and saw her.

"Sweetheart," he said smoothly, covering his surprise.

"I am not your sweetheart," Anne replied coolly. "Nor will I ever be the sweetheart of a man who spreads rumours about me."

He chuckled. "They were not rumours, sweetheart."

She stepped closer to him. "Let me repeat myself. I will happily die an old maid before I will ever consider marrying you."

"A ruined old maid," he muttered. "And everyone will know it. I would not toss my offer to the side so cavalierly if I were you, unless, of course, you wish to remove yourself from society in disgrace."

Her eyes narrowed and had she not been so intently focused on the vile man in front of her, she might have noticed the gentleman, who had earlier cleared his throat at her approach, now frantically waving to Lord Rycroft.

"I assure you, sir," she spat the words out as if they were capable of slapping the gentleman, "that, just as I would I never consider a man who keeps a mistress, I would rather live in disgrace than tie myself to a man who throws his money away on card games because he is too stupid to know he is a poor player." She smiled as his eyes grew wide for a moment. "You thought I did not know about your gaming?" She shook her head. "Then your intelligence is even more limited than even I supposed."

She would have continued, but a hand on her arm stopped her.

"Blackmoore." Rycroft's voice was dangerously gruff. "We are done here. Completely."

Anne looked up at her cousin, who was shaking his head in disgust.

"Do not darken my door," Rycroft continued, "and if I arrive at our club while you are there, you shall do yourself a favour by leaving, or I shall have you removed and banned. Do I make myself clear?" He shook his head again. "What were you thinking? I accept you back after the scheme you attempted on my wife, and you return the favour by importuning my cousin? In my home?"

He cast a look around the group of men that stood with Blackmoore. "If you wish to keep my acquaintance, I suggest that whatever tale was told is never repeated."

While Blackmoore's group of friends each hastily nodded their agreement, he turned back to Blackmoore and motioned toward the door. "Go."

Then, before Blackmoore could say a word, he turned, and with Anne's hand on his arm, strode away – quickly, nearly too quickly for Anne to keep pace with him without scampering.

"Do not look back," he cautioned her in a low voice. "The break must be clear." He slowed his pace a bit as they reached the edge of the ballroom. "I am sorry. I should not have invited him. But, I thought, perhaps... What I was hoping for does not signify. I should not have invited him."

Anne shook her head. "It is I who am sorry. Had I not slipped out that door onto the balcony, you would not have had to cut off a friend. I shall scold myself forever for my stupidity."

Rycroft laughed softly. "I do not think that is necessary, and I fear we may argue a long while and never be satisfied with where the blame should fall. It is likely best if we just share it."

She smiled. "That does seem to be the most logical solution."

"Are you well?" he asked quite seriously.

She nodded. "I am. Thank you."

"You are certain?"

She lifted one shoulder and let it drop. "For the moment."

"Then," he said with a smile, "allow me to remedy that and escort you to your mother."

Anne could not help the laugh that escaped her.

She glanced back once at the ballroom as they moved toward the door. It was nearly empty now, save for servants. Her first ball was over, and at present, she was not sure she ever wished to attend another.

Indeed, she wondered if she would ever be invited to another. Perhaps Mr. Blackmoore and his friends would not speak about the rumours, but what about Miss Ivison?

She shook herself slightly. Tomorrow. Tomorrow would be soon enough to worry about such things. At present, all she wanted was a warm bath and a soft bed. Dancing had been enjoyable but taxing, and that, combined with some of the events of the night, had made her body and mind wearier than they had ever been.

Chapter 5

THE MORNING AFTER RYCROFT's ball, in the middle of the time at which making calls on young ladies – even stubborn ones – was acceptable, Alex swung down from his horse in front of Matlock House and handed the reins to a waiting groom. Then, he took a newspaper and a flask of coffee from his saddlebag and made his way to the door.

He lifted his hand to knock on the door when it opened and a gentleman, whom he did not recognize, exited.

"Good luck to you," the man said with a shake of his head.

"Was it a difficult interview?"

His companion merely chuckled and kept walking.

Alex turned back to the door. "Mr. Madoch to see Miss de Bourgh." He held out his card, which the butler refused with a barely perceivable shake of his head.

"Regretfully, it is my unpleasant business to inform you that Miss de Bourgh is not home to you."

Alex tucked his card away. "I expected as much." He bent to sweep the step with his newspaper and then sat down. Glancing over his shoulder, he saw the butler looking perplexed.

"I will just wait here until she returns," Alex said by way of explanation.

"I believe you misunderstand, sir. She is not home to you and will not be home to you."

"Well, that is to be determined, my good man."

"No, she was quite clear in her instructions. You are not to be admitted."

Alex shrugged and unfolded his paper. "And I was clear last evening when I said I would call on her. That is my intent, and I do not plan to be moved from this spot under my own power until I have gained admittance. Now, if you would be so kind as to go inform the ever-so-obstinate Miss de Bourgh that I am here and will remain here until she sees me." He made a shooing motion with his hand and then turned his attention to his paper.

Behind him, the door closed, and he listened carefully to see if he could make out the sound of a couple strong footmen being summoned to remove him from his perch. No such noise was heard, so Alex opened his flask and took a sip of his somewhat cold coffee which had been mixed with a touch of whiskey to give it some warmth – though he knew the alcohol would not, in truth, warm him.

He was halfway through his flask of coffee and just beginning to read a third article from the paper when the door behind him opened.

"Lady Sophia has agreed to see you," the butler announced.

"Not Miss de Bourgh?" Alex pretended to be disappointed. He was, in fact, pleasantly surprised that he would gain entrance to see anyone. He had expected to spend the whole of calling hours on the step at Matlock House if he were not forcibly removed.

While the thought of being given an audience with the lady whom he knew had been appointed as Anne's advisor was pleasing, he was not so trusting as to believe it impossible for Lady Sophia to simply walk him through the house and out the servants' door. Still, he was hopeful that, at least in the few moments that he might have to speak to her, he would be able to present his suit.

"I am afraid not, sir. It seems Miss de Bourgh is still not home to you. However, if you will follow me, Lady Sophia will see you in the music room."

Alex kept his hat in his hand and his paper under his arm as he followed the butler.

"Mr. Madoch to see you, my lady," the butler said, stepping into the music room ahead of Alex.

Lady Sophia thanked him and rose to greet her guest. "A bit of tea, please, Harrison. A warm cup would be much nicer than whatever you have been partaking of from your flask, would it not?"

"Indeed, it would," Alex agreed.

"You may put your coat and hat there," Lady Sophia motioned to a straight-backed wooden chair that sat near the door. "I promise that you shall not be removed from the house without them." She smiled as she made the comment and motioned for him to take a chair near where she had been sitting. "I gather from your presence here today that you have a desire to marry my niece?"

"I do," Alex said as he casually crossed one leg over the other and rested his elbows on the arms of the chair. "However," he continued, "I fear I do not meet all the published requirements."

Lady Sophia's eyes sparkled with intrigue. "You do not?"

He shook his head. "I have no title, and I am a second son."

Lady Sophia nodded slowly. "But your financial papers are well in order?"

He cocked his head to the side and considered for a moment how much he should tell her. She merely returned his look without wavering as he contemplated her trustworthiness. It only took him a fraction of a minute to decide that if both the admiral and Anne trusted her, then, he could also. He let a sly grin tip his lips as he flicked his eyebrows. "Very well in order, my lady, although I do not have them with me, nor will I be presenting them to Miss de Bourgh for inspection until she has accepted my offer. Of course, I tell you this in the strictest confidence."

Lady Sophia's lips twitched with amusement. "You are very confident to be coming to a meeting knowing you are lacking in some areas and refusing to prove you are not in others."

"Foolishly confident?" he questioned. He needed to know her thinking before he revealed too much of himself.

"That remains to be seen." She rose to pour him a cup of tea as the tea service was set up. "However, I think you just may have what is needed to marry my niece." She put her hand on the teapot and looked up at him. "And it is not anything found in your financial reports."

Alex silently sighed in relief as the music room door opened. It seemed that she would be an ally in his quest.

"Ah, Brother, have you had enough of the conversations in the drawing room? We have just begun an interesting one in here."

Alex stood and bowed to Admiral Fitzwilliam.

"Madoch?" the admiral said in surprise. "What brings you to…" He smiled and clapped his hands together once. "Do not tell me. You are also here to marry my niece."

"He is," Lady Sophia said, "and though my acquaintance with him has been of only a few moments, I would second the notion." She smiled as she handed Alex a cup of tea. "As I said before, I believe you will find this better than what you had been drinking." She arched a brow and gave him a stern look.

"It was coffee, my lady, with just a touch of whiskey to give it the illusion of heat." He took a sip from his cup. "This is infinitely better."

"You are not given to drink, are you?" Lady Sophia busied herself once again with pouring a cup of tea, this time for her brother.

"Not Madoch," the admiral assured her. "Others may indulge but not Madoch. This one always has his wits about him. Shrewd as they come, he is."

Alex gave a small nod in acceptance of the praise. "I thank you for the compliment, sir."

"How is your uncle?" The admiral took a seat and settled in as if he were there for a long chat.

"He is well. His foot pains him occasionally, but it is not enough to do more than slow him. He still insists on being at the stables each day."

Admiral Fitzwilliam turned to his sister. "Thank you," he said as he took the cup of tea she offered. "Madoch's uncle runs the finest stable in all of Brighton."

Alex cleared his throat softly.

Admiral Fitzwilliam chuckled. "Perhaps not the finest. Prinny's is possibly better, eh, Madoch?" He winked at Alex.

Lady Sophia's hand, which was reaching for her own cup of tea, stopped mid-stir. "You know the Prince Regent?"

"Know him?" scoffed the admiral. "This boy runs his stables and his riding school. It is said that Prinny does not make a decision regarding a horse without Madoch's approval."

Lady Sophia dropped into her chair, her tea forgotten. "You sway the opinion of His Highness?"

Alex shook his head. "I do not sway it, my lady. When it comes to horse flesh, I form it."

Lady Sophia's mouth hung open for half a moment before she snapped it shut. "You may not have a title, Mr. Madoch, but you most certainly hold position."

He shrugged. "I do, but for how long? The prince may, at any moment, decide that someone else has better sense, and then where will I be?"

The admiral snorted. "On his own estate, breeding and selling horses is where," he muttered. "Do not let him fool you, Sophia. This one has connections aplenty and money to equal them."

"Is this true?" Lady Sophia's eyes danced with delight.

Alex leaned forward in his chair and lowered his voice. "What the admiral says is true; however, Miss de Bourgh is not to know about it." He held his breath, hoping that Lady Sophia and Admiral Fitzwilliam would not ruin his plans to win Anne's heart without revealing the particulars of his situation.

Confusion replaced the delight in Lady Sophia's eyes. "Why ever not? She will refuse to consider you without knowing of your qualifications."

"Because I wish for her to choose me. Not my wealth. Not my connections. Me." He held Lady Sophia's gaze. "I wish for her to follow her heart."

Lady Sophia's eyes grew wide as understanding dawned on her. "You love her? But how?"

Alex released his breath quickly. "My father's estate is in Kent, near Rosings." He paused, not sure how much of his story he should share.

"This family is good at keeping secrets," Lady Sophia encouraged while casting a quick glance at her brother.

"Aye," the admiral agreed, "from the world and each other." He winked at his sister.

"Can you assure me that not a word of my situation will be shared with Miss de Bourgh?"

"Not a word," Lady Sophia agreed.

"Will you allow her to walk away from me if that is her choice?"

Lady Sophia was silent for a moment. "Yes, I will allow it unless in doing so she will be utterly miserable." She shook her head. "I cannot allow that." She smiled reassuringly at him. "Perhaps the knowledge I gain from your tale will assist me in knowing how best to help."

"My sister, the matchmaker," the admiral said as he waved his hand toward his sister with a flourish. "She'll not rest, my boy, until things have been arranged to best advantage."

Alex could not help the chuckle that escaped him. "Very well. Then, I shall tell you."

Chapter 6

"I WAS NOT DONE with my schooling – about halfway through my studies of the law – when I met her." Alex took a sip of his tea. "I had visited several stables in the area surrounding my father's estate. Each time I came home for a visit, I would revisit one or find another to tour for the first time. I never intended to take up the law profession. I had set my mind to the study to help me when it came to writing contracts and conducting deals."

The admiral chuckled. "I told you he was shrewd," he muttered.

"Shh," Lady Sophia scolded. "Tell me about your meeting."

For the next ten minutes, Alex told of his interest in the stables at Rosings and of the young girl of fourteen who had sneaked into those very stables in search of a fast horse, one that was quick enough to cause her troubles to float away on the wind.

In his mind's eye, Alex saw the red rims of Anne's eyes and heard her soft sniffle as the groom readied a steady mare.

⟆⟊⟋

"She is not fast enough," the delicate but distraught young miss grumbled.

"She is the only horse you are allowed, miss," the stable master explained. "I'll not risk my position or your life. I dare say I risk enough by allowing you to ride when your mother is unaware." He gave Anne a stern look.

Anne huffed. She pulled her arms more tightly around her waist, as if trying to hold her hurt inside. She stood silently shifting from foot to foot and watching a cat swish his *tail* back and forth as he sat perched on a stool.

"Henry will ride with you." The stable master took the reins from the groom and led the horse out to where the steps had been put in place to help Anne in mounting the mare.

"Mr. Madoch," he called over his shoulder, "you may also attend Miss de Bourgh. It will give you the chance you have been wanting to see our horses in action. I will be interested to hear what you have to say about their quality when you return."

Anne looked at Alex, who was leaning against the side of the stable.

"Miss de Bourgh." The stable master stood ready to assist her in mounting. "That is the younger Mr. Madoch," he explained.

Alex pulled himself straight and bowed.

Anne's brows furrowed. "I know who he is. I have seen him at church. Why is he here?"

"He has an interest in horses," the stable master continued.

"Does he not have one of his own?" She scowled at him.
Clearly, she did not want him to ride with her.

"I will not trouble you, Miss de Bourgh, unless you wish
it." Alex smiled at her.

"Why are you not at school?" she asked. Her tone was
decidedly displeased.

"I return Monday next," he said, swinging neatly into
his seat.

"What are you studying?" Anne asked.

"Law." He was studying it, but he had no desire to
pursue it. His interests were entirely wrapped up in horses,
but his father insisted that he study a proper profession.
And so, thinking that the law might help him in his future
dealing with customers and landowners, he had taken up
the study of the law and had excelled enough to please his
father.

Anne chewed her lip as if it might help her figure out
whatever it was that had caused her distress while Alex
rode silently next to her. Silence was not easy to maintain,
especially when, from time to time, she would cast a cautious glance at him.

❦

"I had intended to remain silent and merely observe the
horses, but after she had looked my direction the fourth
time, I spoke. I told her about my love of horses and my
plans to one day own my own stable." He smiled. "And so
started a friendship. When I was home, I spent more and

more time at Rosings. We rode together and discussed all that was both right and wrong in our worlds. She eventually told me that an argument between her parents had sent her to the stables on the day we met." Hers was not an easy life.

"She was just set to be given a season in town the last time I saw her," Alex continued. "She was nineteen, and I was afraid she would be whisked away by some gentleman as soon as she set foot in town." He paused and looked at his hands. "So, I spoke to her about my desire to marry."

Lady Sophia gasped, while the admiral sighed and shook his head. "I take it, since we are here discussing your desire to be her husband today, that the discussion did not go well?"

Alex chuckled bitterly. "To put it gently. I had met with her in the stable as was our wont, and taking her by the hands, I presented my offer..."

⁓⁓❦⁓⁓

"Marry you?" Anne asked in surprise, pulling her hands away from him.

"Yes."

"I cannot marry you." Anne turned her back to him. "In truth, I am not ready to sign my life away to anyone, but you? You are *a second* son with little inheritance. Your father is no one of importance while my father is a baronet and my uncle is *an earl*." She turned back toward him. Her eyes shimmered with unshed tears, and her lips trembled.

He would bet all he would ever own that she was not so unattached to him as she was attempting to portray. He had always been excellent at reading horses and nearly as good at deciphering people.

"But I will be a man of substance one day, Anne. Earls and even dukes, if not the king himself, will seek me out." He did not plan to be content with some non-descript life. He planned to be the best at what he did. He had to be. His father's opinion mattered to him – nearly as much as the opinion of the lady in front of him did.

She laughed coldly. It was a painfully sharp sound and one that seemed foreign coming from her.

"You?" she scoffed. "You must be mad. People of rank do not seek out people like you. They use them, manipulate them, and cast them aside. I want no part of that!" She clenched her jaw tightly and shrugged. "You are not good enough." She had pressed her lips firmly together, swiped quickly at a tear which had rolled down her cheek, nodded a goodbye, and fled from him.

⟡

Alex blew out a breath and sat quietly for a moment at the end of his recitation of the events of that day. The harshness of her refusal had taken him by surprise, and it had torn his heart in pieces. However, he had known then, just as he knew now, that she had loved him, and he was nearly certain she still loved him as much as he loved her. But she was like a scared filly – skittish and wary, with a temper that would flare to protect herself. He only hoped he would be able to convince her that her fears were unfounded if she chose to trust him.

"This is why I must insist that you not tell her of my position," he said, breaking the silence in the room. "I have risen to what she would not believe back then that I could be, and I assure you that my affairs are such that I cannot be cast aside." He straightened a bit. "In fact, it is I who am now able to cast aside if I so choose. My opinions and advice are not given unless I decide they should be shared." He smiled wryly. "Unless, of course, you are the Prince Regent. I find it difficult to put him off very often."

Once again, the room fell silent. Finally, Lady Sophia stood and said, "I shall not share a word." A smile spread across her face and a scheming glint shone in her eyes. "However, that does not mean I will not promote you to her. Are you going to the Hamilton's musicale?"

"I had not thought to," Alex replied.

Lady Sophia shook her head. "Are you going to the Hamilton's musicale?"

Alex nodded slowly. "I am?"

Lady Sophia clapped her hands in delight. "Excellent, so are we."

"I suspect, my boy, that there will be a chair available for you next to my niece," the admiral said with a chuckle.

Lady Sophia shrugged and winked. "I cannot promise, but I would be delighted if you would *happen* join us. This has been such a pleasant interview, in which I learned as much as I could. You are a fine gentleman and worthy of consideration. Financially sound, hardworking, respected, and whatever other descriptors I might find between now and when I speak to Anne."

Alex blinked, somewhat confused by the way in which Lady Sophia was speaking.

The admiral threw an arm around Alex's shoulder. "What do you say we sneak out the back entrance and take a walk so that I can attempt to explain the workings of my sister's mind?"

"That might speed up the process for me," Alex agreed and went to get his hat and coat.

Admiral Fitzwilliam held the door for him to exit. "Firstly, she cannot invite you to join her because if Anne asks, she will be forced to either tell the truth, which she does not wish to have revealed, or lie, which she does not want to do. And before you ask it, no, she is not concealing anything because she never invited you."

Alex glanced at Lady Sophia who tapped her nose, indicating her brother was correct, and then poured herself a fresh cup of tea as the door closed behind Alex and the admiral.

Chapter 7

ANNE CAST A GLANCE at the sitting room door when it opened to allow Lady Sophia entrance. Her eyes wandered to the clock, and she wondered at the length of time of time her aunt had been gone from the room. Had it been more than a quarter hour? She was almost certain it had been. It should not have taken more than a few moments to see that Mr. Madoch was removed from the front of the house and reminded that he was not to put forward a suit. Sadly, he was not a suitable candidate. Perhaps she needed to make those facts plain to her aunt once again.

Yes, she would do just that as soon as she finished with Sir Hugh — she looked at the papers in her lap — Mattingly. She tilted her head to the side. Lady Anne Mattingly. That sounded very acceptable. She turned her attention to Sir Hugh's documents once again.

He was not wealthy beyond measure, but he was solvent and substantially so. She flipped through the papers, looking at his holdings and financial records. Then, she placed them in the stack that was slowly building on the table next to her.

She looked carefully at the gentleman before her. He was not plain. In fact, his face was very like those created from marble by a master sculptor's hand. He held himself with dignity under her scrutiny and merely smiled. That could be a weakness, she noted. He might be far too self-assured to be pleasant. She leaned forward, feigning a need to fix something on her shoe.

"It is such an annoyance when one's slipper catches on one's dress." She had inhaled deeply as she had reached for her foot. He smelled very pleasant. She marked off good hygiene on her mental list. So far, he seemed a very likely candidate.

"Sir Hugh," she said, situating herself back in a proper upright position. "You are a knight, not a baronet, is that correct?"

"It is, indeed, Miss de Bourgh."

"And how did it come to be that you were given the title?" Knighthoods were not inherited, after all.

"There was a matter of some money owed that was forgiven, and as a sign of gratitude, the title was bestowed."

"Do you gamble?" That would be a sad thing, she was beginning to like looking at him and his voice was very pleasant.

"On occasion, but never more than I can afford and always when His Highness demands it."

She raised an eyebrow and contemplated that. "Are you often with the prince?"

"No, no, I have only been invited to play with him a handful of times."

A handful was not so many, but then, to be included in a group so close to the prince did have its merits. It was not as if Sir Hugh had been born to such rank and privilege.

"You say you never wager to excess?" She needed reassurance. Debt was a very easy way for a man, and therefore, his whole family, to fall under the power of another.

"Never. My estate and legacy are far too valuable to risk on an evening's entertainment."

She smiled and relaxed just a bit. He did seem to know the proper answer to give. "And in what other forms of entertainment do you partake? The theatre? Concerts? Riding?"

"I do enjoy an invigorating ride either on horseback or in a curricle and would be most honoured if I were allowed to escort you to the park on a drive."

A drive in the park? Oh, that sounded lovely! He was the first gentleman to ask it of her. But was it wise? Would it raise his expectations too much? There were still things she did not know about him. However, the smile he wore did make the offer hard to resist.

"I think I would like that; however, and you must forgive me for being so forward, there are still two vices about which I must question you."

He chuckled, and Anne suddenly became less concerned with his uprightness and a good deal more eager to drive through the park with him.

"I do not drink to excess," he said. "And I would never consider a mistress after I was married unless my wife made it necessary."

Anne's eyes grew wide, and she blushed at what he implied, which made him smirk. It was a somewhat annoying expression, but it was also quite handsome.

"Do I pass, Miss de Bourgh? May I take you for a drive tomorrow?"

Anne bit her lip and furrowed her brow as if in deep thought. Then after what she deemed was an appropriate length of time for consideration, gave a small nod of her head and extended her hand. "You have succeeded so far as a ride is concerned. We are not yet acquainted well enough to determine if your suit shall succeed above all."

He took her hand and instead of shaking it as she had extended it for him to do, he turned it and placed a kiss gently on her knuckles.

My! Where was one's fan when one needed it?

"Until tomorrow at five, then, Miss de Bourgh," he said as he rose.

"Yes, until then."

Anne tipped her head to the side and allowed her eyes to follow him all the way to the door of the sitting room. He cut quite a stirring figure as he left the room, and since all the other hopeful gentleman had left, she did not bother to check her pleasure at watching him leave.

"He is quite acceptable, I think," she said to Lady Sophia when the front door to Matlock House had closed behind Sir Hugh.

"He is rather attractive," her aunt said from her place of observation to the left of Anne.

Rather attractive was not giving his appearance the credit it was due, but Anne was not certain she should say such, so instead, she picked up his financial reports. "And he is both titled and wealthy."

"He seems practiced." There was a note of caution in her aunt's tone.

"He is two and thirty, Aunt Sophia. I expect a man of such an age has had his share of experience in speaking to a woman." She knew what her aunt was talking about, but she did not want to consider at this moment that the handsome and charming Sir Hugh was anything less than acceptable.

Lady Sophia huffed. "Not as smoothly as he spoke to you. *I* do not trust him, and I think you should take care, but despite my misgivings, I shall allow you to take a drive with him tomorrow. You must remember, however, that it is your uncle and I who have the final word as to whether he is acceptable." She dipped her head to the side and her eyes held Anne's in a demanding stare. "That means that he must impress not only you but us as well."

Anne sighed heavily.

"I love you, Anne," her aunt said softly. "I do not wish for you to be unhappy, and if I fear Sir Hugh will shower you with pretty words now and neglect you later, I will not approve of him. I have seen more of the world than you, my dear. I am not opposed to your seeing it, but I am opposed you being hurt by it."

Anne nodded her understanding. What else could she do when the aunt she loved spoke so fervently about caring for her?

"What did you think of Sir Hugh, Catherine?" Lady Sophia turned toward Anne's mother, who was still in the room but had been only allowed to have a chair in the far corner.

Anne had not wanted her mother hovering. Truth be told, she had not wanted her mother present at all. However, that was a battle she had not felt like engaging in today, and so she had granted her a place in the room from which to watch the proceedings. It had been a good thing, too, after all, when Lady Sophia had been required to deal with Mr. Madoch.

"Oh, he seemed a fine choice. Quite handsome with a charming smile and amiable personality, and do not forget he has a title – minor though it is," her mother effused. "I would not mind him for a son at all."

Anne scowled. Her mother approved of him? That was most definitely a strike against the man.

Lady Catherine rose to look out the window, leaning close to peer at the equipage making its way down the street. "He has a fine carriage and horses. It would make for a comfortable ride to and from Kent and wherever else his estate might be."

"Mother, I am not selecting a driver. I am choosing a husband."

"Oh, yes, yes," Lady Catherine turned back toward Anne. "I know what you are doing, my dear. But you will need an elegant carriage in which to ride. Travel can be a strain and with your ill health..."

"My health is not a concern." She narrowly refrained from adding that her health had never truly been poor. Maladies had come and gone as needed to keep her free from her mother and so she could enjoy her time as she pleased. "I find I have never felt so well in all my life. It must be all the activity and splendour of the season."

Lady Catherine gave a disapproving snort. "If you keep too busy a schedule, you will soon find yourself once again in need of a doctor. I think you would do well to keep to your room for the evening. A long rest would see you certain to impress Sir Hugh on the morrow." She looked around the room and waved her arm in an encompassing motion. "Will there be more of these calls?"

Why could her mother not show a fraction of the care that Lady Sophia did? It seemed to Anne that her mother was only interested in having this ordeal of gentleman callers over with and her daughter ensconced in the best carriage one could buy, but then, what one possessed had always been of most importance to her mother. Therefore, she should not be surprised by her mother's actions. It was, after all, the reason she knew that she could not just marry as she wanted to marry but had to be so careful in her selection of a husband.

"There will be more calls if more gentlemen come." The sharp pain Anne felt in her heart coloured her tone. "I shall not just accept the first seemingly agreeable gentleman and be off to Gretna Green."

"I should hope not!" Lady Catherine cried. "My heavens! What a scandal that would be! It is bad enough that you have advertised for a husband. Were you to hie off to Scotland, there would be no hope of establishing yourself in polite society." She shook her head. "I cannot imagine what a gentleman is thinking by presenting himself to a lady as if he is a sample that needs to be purchased. Financial concerns should be left to the men. It is the way of things."

"Yes, Mother." Anne spoke through clenched teeth. She wished to point out to her mother that having a gentleman present his assets and credentials was not so different from a lady learning to dance and sing and perform so that she might be seen as an acceptable choice, but she knew that would only lead to a long and protracted argument and a sizeable headache. Neither were things she wished to endure, so instead she gave her aunt an imploring look. "Would it not be best if we were to retire to my apartment to review the particulars of each caller?"

"I think that is an excellent idea." Lady Sophia rose along with Anne and then followed her from the room.

Chapter 8

"MAY I SEE THE papers you have collected?" Lady Sophia asked Anne as they entered her sitting room.

"Of course." Anne made her way to her favourite settee and, sitting down, removed her slippers. "You were gone for quite some time with Mr. Madoch."

Her aunt looked up from reading the papers and smiled. "He looked cold, so I offered him some tea to ward off any dangers from being chilled. I would not want him to become ill." She returned to her perusal of the financial reports she held.

"Is that all?"

This time her aunt did not lift her eyes from their task as she replied. "We had a lovely conversation along with the tea if that is what you wish to know."

Anne wanted to ask her aunt what they had talked about, but that seemed like it would make her seem more interested in Alex than she should be.

"Your uncle joined us, and then he and Mr. Madoch left together. It seems they know one another – at least in passing – from the time the admiral has spent in various seaside locales. He is quite a lovely young man. It really is too bad that he did not bring any documents like these with him."

Anne laughed. "What would he put on them? That he is a second son with little fortune?"

Her aunt's eyes sparkled with amusement. "Perhaps. He struck me as the very direct sort."

That he was. There was no pretense with Alex. What he said, he did, and what he thought was not hidden any more than it was required to be in certain situations. If only he had a title and a fortune!

"You can place those on this table when you are done," Anne suggested, "and we can sort them into three piles — acceptable and worthy of pursuing, potentially suitable and worthy of a second consideration, and without doubt, never to be considered again."

Lady Sophia held the papers out to her. "I am afraid I am not able to judge your opinion. That being said, the acceptable and those just missing acceptance will need to be reviewed by your uncle and me."

"Yes, I know." Anne rose, took the papers from her aunt, and began sorting. Goodness! There really were not many to put in the first two categories. It seemed it would be much harder to find a husband she would not mind spending the rest of her life with than she had supposed. That was not a very encouraging thought.

"There do not seem to be many of whom you approve," Lady Sophia said as she settled into a chair at the table. "Indeed, it appears that most of your callers were con-temptible."

Anne sighed. "They are all so boring." As interesting as a wall in an art gallery without a single painting on or near it.

She pulled herself straight and wagged her head from side to side before standing and speaking in an imitation of a dull gentleman. "Miss de Bourgh, as you can see, my financial reports are in good order." She selected one of the papers from the not-to-be considered pile and handed it to her aunt. "My father has seen to it that my education is good and the title to which I will ascend is well protected. There shall not be a want of security – not for my estate, not for yourself, and not for our offspring. In fact, my title and my estate have been secure for many years."

She dropped back onto her chair and looked at her aunt in exasperation. "And then they would prattle on about their family's history and the number of sons that had been born and daughters that had been advantageously married. I did not need a history lesson at this meeting, but it seems they thought I did."

She shook her head and returned to sorting. "I tried to stop some of them from proceeding, but it was to no avail. It was like speaking to my mother!" Here she allowed herself a very unladylike growl. There was no way in this world that she would ever consider someone as a husband if they reminded her of her mother!

"And do you know what they did when I asked them about amusements?"

"I am sure I could not say," Lady Sophia replied.

"They had to think for several minutes before they could share an original thought that had not been given to them by their fathers. How does one not know what one likes to do without being told one likes it?"

She placed the last paper in a pile and rose to cross the room "Sir Hugh was the first to offer anything remotely interesting by way of a drive. Not one of the other gentlemen thought to do so. It was as if they did not enjoy speaking to me at all. It was as if meeting me were a mere formality that must be completed."

Lady Sophia chuckled softly as Anne flung herself onto the settee.

"I do not see what is so humorous about it!" she grumbled.

"I find it a trifle amusing that you find *what you requested* to be not at all *what you want*."

Anne sat up. "What do you mean?"

"Your advertisement requested a responsible first-born son – an heir with a fortune, a title, and proper conduct. As usually happens, the more adventurous, and therefore, less dull, heir is a gentleman who is often given to wild ways and excesses which do not lead to financial soundness or particularly virtuous behaviour. Allow me to present Mr. Blackmoore as an excellent example of an undesirable, yet interesting, heir. He is not dull, but he is also not suitable."

That was true. Mr. Blackmoore was not the sort of heir for whom she was looking, but certainly there must be some gentleman somewhere who fit her requirements and was not completely uninteresting. Perhaps —

"Lord Brownlow is not a bore, but he did not present a file. He came merely as a friend." She sighed and draped an arm across her eyes, blocking out the light that was beginning to increase the small pain in her head. "I wish he would have brought his papers. I quite like him, and a lord is better than a sir."

"That it is," Lady Sophia agreed. "Perhaps you should expand your search to include those without a title? It is not the title a gentleman holds that brings the security of a stable home and finances."

"But it brings power," Anne protested. And power was important. "It means that the man in possession of that title has sway over another merely because of his title."

She thought of many of the arguments she had overheard as a child. How many of them had ended with "*but you must remember who my brother is.*" This had always been followed by her father doing whatever it was that he had not wished to do simply because it *would not do* to offend the Earl of Matlock.

She had seen the sadness in his posture and the dimming of the light in his eyes. Her heart had broken for her dear father a little bit more each time she had witnessed it, and she was convinced that it was that constant battering of his pride which had led to his finally succumbing to illness – perhaps not altogether, but in part.

"You are not wrong," her aunt agreed. "A title can give power, but it is not the only thing that can, my dear."

Anne lifted her arm and peeked at her aunt, from whom she received a gentle and understanding smile.

"A lowly man with no title can become quite powerful when he has the one thing that is needed by many — be it money or safety or food," her aunt explained. "And a great man can be controlled by those to whom he owes money. While a man of little feelings for anyone save himself can be powerful due to his cruelty, and a person who possesses knowledge of that which you fear most can sway you with little effort." She shook her head sadly. "My sweet Anne, we cannot guarantee that another will not at some point try to bend us to his will – no matter our standing. Remember what happened in France to those who were of the aristocracy."

Anne shook her head. How was she to find safety and security when so many things threatened? Was it truly impossible?

"Do not look at their title, my dear niece. Look at their character. A man with few worldly possessions but with integrity is better than a king with great wealth and no conscience."

Her smile turned teasing as she rose from where she was sitting. "Do not be alarmed, but I am going to agree with your mother and suggest you have a short rest. We have a musicale to attend, and I would not wish for you to fall asleep during the performance."

She walked over to Anne and held out her hand. "Come. You need a proper rest. Lying here in such a position will only give you a stiff neck and a foul mood."

Anne looked at her aunt's hand for a moment before she took it and rose to her feet. If only all those who held titles were so willing to offer help as Lady Sophia was.

Before allowing her to go to her bedchamber, Lady Sophia drew Anne into her embrace. "I think you are wise to see to your financial future. Very wise. A lady should not blithely dance into her future in that area, but she must also not forget everything else that makes a gentleman a good husband while conducting her analysis of his bank account and holdings. Promise me you will consider what I have said."

Anne squeezed her aunt close and nodded against her shoulder as a tear slipped down her cheek. She could feel the love of her aunt wrapping itself around her mind and heart as tightly as her aunt's arms held her close.

"I will," she promised.

Chapter 9

ANNE'S UNCLE, THE ADMIRAL, stood at the end of a row of chairs while she and her aunt, Lady Sophia, took their seats among the other guests in the Hamiltons' music room.

"These two chairs –" Her uncle indicated the two next to Anne. "Are not to be given away." He raised a brow and gave both Anne and Lady Sophia a hard stare.

To Anne, both the request and the glare were a bit odd. "Of course," she said.

Lady Sophia smiled and made herself comfortable while saying, "Then, be quick, for I will not be held responsible for giving away your seats if a handsome young man or two need them."

"I will not be any longer than is necessary," the admiral said before hurrying away as if he were on a mission to secure the final piece of apple cake on a platter. Her uncle did enjoy a sweet treat, especially cake.

"This is my first musicale of the season." Lady Sophia's excitement at the thought was evident in her tone. "If only you played, it would give you quite the stage from which to draw attention from the gentlemen present."

"I do not like performing," Anne said quickly. "There are too many eyes watching the performer, and most of them are looking to find fault." She shuddered. She had had enough flaws pointed out to her by her mother over the years. She did not need to give strangers an opportunity to do so. "I would not play even if I could."

She turned and took a hasty survey of the room. It was filling quickly. Gentlemen stood around the edges of the it, watching as the ladies and their chaperones arrived — looking, she supposed, for the best choice of listening partner. She laughed to herself and wondered if it was much like this, minus the fine evening clothes, when the gentlemen gathered at Tattersall's.

However, she thought as she took in her surroundings, the furnishings and carpet here must certainly be better than those found at a horse auction.

And my! Was not the room beautifully arranged? Rows of chairs with tufted cream-coloured cushions faced a large, rounded alcove where a pianoforte stood next to a harp. Both instruments had a deep reddish hue and had obviously been carefully polished because they both shone beneath the light of the large chandelier that hung overhead. If one had to embarrass themselves with a performance, Anne was certain there could be no place more beautiful for doing it. She was just glad that she was not among the debutantes that would be called on to entertain.

She was so caught up in looking at the people and splendour of the room that she nearly missed her uncle's return with the friend for whom he had been waiting. She glanced to her left as the admiral took his seat and had just returned her eyes to the painting above the fireplace when her mind grasped who had joined them. Her eyes grew wide at the thought, and her heart thumped loudly beneath the ruffles of her dress.

"Aunt Sophia." She leaned close to her aunt and grasped her arm firmly. "He is in the pile of unacceptable choices."

"No, he is not, my dear. You have not received his portfolio."

Anne glared at her aunt. "For good reason," she muttered.

Her aunt patted the hand that gripped her arm. "Smile and be polite, dear. There are many from the acceptable pile who will be watching. It would do you no good to be thought of as cold and aloof. Besides, Mr. Madoch is a friend of your uncle, and I am sure you would not wish to offend your uncle."

Well, no, she did not want to do that. She loved her uncle far too dearly to wish to offend him, but did she truly have to sit next to Alex to avoid doing so? She leaned toward her aunt once and again and whispered, "Then, may I switch seats with you, so that I do not?"

Lady Sophia laughed and bent to look around her. "It is a pleasure to see you this evening, Mr. Madoch. Is it not, Anne?" She gave her niece a pointed look.

"Indeed, it must be if my aunt says so," Anne replied, turning to greet Alex.

Oh, he was handsome in his blue coat – drat him! And he smelled of cinnamon, mingled with other spices, which only made things worse. He had always smelled of cinnamon. For the longest time after she had refused him, every cup of mulled cider, every spiced cake or biscuit had caused her stomach to knot and clench with regret.

No, no, she told herself, it was not regret. It was... she tapped her finger on her leg trying to think of the best way to describe it to herself so that she would not think of her refusal of him as anything more than what should have happened. He was not acceptable because...

She looked at him as he spoke to her aunt. He did not look like a poor ne'er-do-well. That was unfortunate because if he did, then, she could dismiss him as such. He caught her eye and smiled that smile at her again, just as he had on the balcony of Rycroft Place, and she felt her resolve slip again just as it had then.

He was unacceptable, she reminded herself, because...

Because he is, she concluded. She would spend time later listing the reasons he was to remain off her list of marital candidates. Had he just complimented her?

"I said you look lovely this evening, Miss de Bourgh. That shade of pink has always been well-suited to your complexion."

He *had* complimented her and so sweetly – of all the rotten things for him to do! Gentlemen were not supposed to know if a colour suited your complexion, were they? She narrowed her eyes at the thought. Perhaps he *was* just saying what he thought should be said. That, she thought to herself, was quite acceptable, was it not?

"I have always told her so, myself," her aunt said while using her elbow to give Anne's side a light tap.

It was true. Not only had Aunt Sophia complimented her on her dress, but both Lord and Lady Matlock had as well. She sighed. Alex was not given to pretense. She knew this.

"Thank you, Mr. Madoch."

Her aunt's elbow poked her side again.

"You also look well this evening," she added.

He lifted one shoulder in a faint shrug and gave himself an appraising look. "I do know how to clean up, I suppose."

She rolled her eyes without thinking. He had always had a certain amount of swagger about him. He had never been one to over or understate himself. Well, perhaps he had inflated his value when he claimed that the king would one day look to him for advice, but, beyond that, he been quite accurate in his assessments of his abilities.

"I was not aware that you were a friend of my uncle." At least, she had not been until her aunt had mentioned it earlier.

"To be entirely accurate, the admiral is a friend of my uncle, and I have the good fortune of being my uncle's nephew and that has earned me a coveted spot as a friend of Admiral Fitzwilliam." There was a twinkle in his eye, and the comment received the response Anne was certain it was designed to elicit as the admiral guffawed and slapped Mr. Madoch on the back.

"Do not let him fool you, Anne. He has been as much a friend to me as his uncle has. You cannot find a better man to speak all things horse to you, you know. And even an old sailor like me wants a reliable mount when he is on land. No one knows more about horses than Madoch, and he is always good for a friendly game of some sort — no wagers allowed, however. He is not one to part with his money unnecessarily."

Anne noticed a faint blush creeping above the edge of Alex's cravat. The sight of it surprised her. He was not one to be embarrassed. The tone of his voice in expressing his thanks for the kind words was also new to her.

It seemed that he truly cared what her uncle thought of him. This picture clashed with the often-brash persona he had demonstrated when she knew him before. But then, people changed over time, and it had been six years.

"Are you performing?" Alex asked in a whisper as a young lady sat down at the pianoforte and began a short piece which was intended to call them to order. "I know you do not play, but you sing quite well. I have missed the tunes you would sing to the horses. My horse does not enjoy my renditions as much as he did yours."

Anne gave him a small smile but said nothing since the programme was beginning. As Miss Hamilton began to play and sing an Irish air, Anne's thoughts were filled with his words. He had missed her. His words had said it almost as much as his tone. The thought did nothing to comfort her. In fact, it increased that knotting of her stomach caused by something that was *definitely not* regret, although she had yet to decide on what it was.

As the night progressed, young ladies played and sang. Some did so with great enjoyment, glowing in the applause that followed and reluctantly returning to their seats, while others performed as if it was something that was a necessary task but one which held very little, if any, satisfaction. This second group of ladies would take their places quickly and begin with no more than a glance at the audience. Then, as soon as the last note faded, they wasted no time in returning to their chairs. Some performances were delightful while some were truly painful.

By the end of the evening, Anne's cheeks were sore from smiling as she politely clapped for each performance and when she spoke about the weather and this dress and that hat with the various people around her. And all that was mingled with the wonderful, yet torturous, presence of the man next to her, whom she longed for with all her heart, despite telling herself several times that he was not acceptable.

To say she was relieved and delighted when, at last, she was able to exit the Hamiltons' and make her way towards Lady Sophia's coach was stating things mildly. She was, in fact, overjoyed by the prospect of the rest that awaited her in her bed at home. However, her escape to the awaiting bliss was not to be a smooth one, for just as Lady Sophia's carriage had pulled forward and a footman was about to put the steps in place...

"Miss de Bourgh," Sir Hugh said as he approached her, "I had hoped to see you here tonight, but alas, I was delayed and by the time I arrived, the intermission had passed, and, with such a crush of people, it was impossible to make my way to you. I am very glad that I have not missed you entirely."

Anne pulled her tired facial muscles into another smile. It was not that she did not wish to see or speak to Sir Hugh, but she was tired, and her nerves were feeling the effects of the evening. "I am glad you were not disappointed."

Having gained Anne's welcome, Sir Hugh turned to the others in her party, greeting first her aunt and then her uncle.

"Madoch," he said with a tip of his head. "I had heard you were in town."

Chapter 10

"ARE YOU ENJOYING THE season?" Sir Hugh gave Alex what he would call an appraising look, so Alex returned it in kind.

"I have enjoyed the two soirees that I have attended." Alex had no desire to speak with Sir Hugh on the best of days, and he particularly did not wish to speak to him now. Nor did he like the way the man had smiled so fondly while talking to Anne or how Anne had so readily returned his smile.

"Do you know each other?" Anne's eyes blinked rapidly as if the thought of his knowing someone like Sir Hugh was startling to her.

"Oh, indeed," Sir Hugh replied, as if the question were one that had quite the obvious answer, which to most it was – though not to Anne. "Not many a fellow does not know Madoch if he has an interest in horses – and who of the gentry or nobility do not have such an interest? In fact, the horses, which will take us through the park tomorrow on our drive, I purchased on his recommendation, and they are a handsome pair. I think you will easily agree when you see them."

Alex did not miss how Anne's brows furrowed, and he was certain that she was attempting to piece together what she had heard with what she knew of him.

"But Mr. Madoch is in Brighton. Do you often travel to the coast just to learn about which horses to purchase?" Anne asked Sir Hugh.

"I am not always in Brighton, and there is always the mail," Alex replied before Sir Hugh had a chance to utter a word.

"Yes, quite right," Sir Hugh agreed. "I admit that I met Mr. Madock once in Brighton a few years back, but when it came to buying my horses, I merely wrote to him for advice."

Anne tilted her head to the side and looked at Alex with her brows still drawn closely together in confusion. "How can anyone recommend a horse through a letter? Do you not need to see the creatures to know if they are good or not?"

"I had seen them," Alex answered. "And the breeder is reputable. There was no need to doubt that they had been well cared for between when I last saw them and when Sir Hugh sent his inquiry. I had facilitated sales from the seller before with pleasing results."

"Indeed?" Anne's brows rose in surprise. "Were they purchased by your uncle?"

"No. Someone else." He shifted uneasily. While he was pleased that she now knew he was held in high esteem by some, she did not need to know that the horses he now spoke of were numbered among those of the riding school at Brighton. Knowing he was an esteemed businessman would not be enough to make her consider him merely for his position, and he was still determined that she choose him because her heart demanded it, not because he met some ridiculous standard of acceptance.

"Who?"

"Not all the sales I broker are a matter of public record," Alex answered as coolly as he could, hoping that his tone would put an end to this conversation. It was true that not all the sales or purchases in which he had a hand were a matter with which society need be concerned. However, the ones about which he was refusing to talk had been made known publicly.

"Oh, of course." Anne's smile was tight, and Alex cursed the success of his sharp reply.

"Forgive my impertinence," she continued before shivering.

The air was not warm, but Alex wasn't sure if it was the ambient temperature of their surroundings or his reply which had caused the shiver. The Anne he knew was proficient at hiding any sign of weakness.

"Miss de Bourgh, you must not catch a chill." Sir Hugh extended his hand to help her to her carriage.

"Very true," Lady Sophia agreed. "You have a busy schedule of outings and soirees. I would not wish you to miss them on account of standing outside in the night air for too long a period."

Anne hesitated a moment before accepting Sir Hugh's assistance. However, she kept a smile on her lips as she dipped a small parting curtsey to Alex and allowed herself to be escorted to and handed into her carriage. Still, he was going to take that hesitation and the backwards glance in his direction as she entered the carriage as signs that he might eventually find success for his quest.

"You have her confused," the admiral said in a soft voice as he made a show of saying his farewells. "I understand a ride in Hyde Park around five in the evening is the time to see and be seen, or so my sister tells me. I may venture out there myself *tomorrow* to test her theory." He gave Alex a wink and then, chuckling, turned toward the carriage.

Alex shook his head at the admiral's meddling. First, he had flattered Alex in such a way as to tell his niece of Alex's dislike of gambling and his seriousness in considering finances. Now, Admiral Fitzwilliam was suggesting a bit more subterfuge in creating a meeting in the park. He chuckled as he went to find his horse. It seemed Lady Sophia was not the only matchmaker in the family.

"Have you made any inroads?" Jonathan, who had not attended tonight's soiree and who was never anywhere unexpected without a reason, sat on his horse next to where a groom held Alex's.

Alex swung up onto his mount before motioning with his head for his friend to follow him. "Why have you come looking for me?"

"I am curious."

Alex laughed. "No, you are not. You are the least curious person I know. So why?"

"Have you made any progress with Miss de Bourgh?"

"I believe I have. Now, why are you here?

"I heard something."

Alex slowed his horse and drew closer to his friend. "And why is this something of importance to me?" There was no other reason for Jonathan to have tracked him down. It was not as if the fellow was a gossip eager to share tales just for the pleasure of telling the tale.

"It seems that someone has talked the termagant into leaving her lair and going for a ride."

Alex nodded. "I know. Sir Hugh mentioned it this evening."

"You know he cheats."

"Yes, I am aware of that fact. It is why I do not play with him unless I can help it and have money to lose." He sighed. "Why are you telling me things that I already know?"

"He wants her money." Jonathan said it softly and slowly and then just let the idea hang in the air without adding to it.

Alex closed his eyes as the facts fell into place. He had never liked Sir Hugh. Yes, Alex had given him advice about some excellent horses, but that was business. It profited Alex and kept the scoundrel from seeking ways to harass him as he had done with others.

"How?" If anyone knew the plot that was being planned, it would be Jonathan, for he was dreadfully good at being both inconspicuous and attentive.

"That was not agreed upon by the gentlemen I heard. Some think he will force her hand, while others think he will either buy off or spread misinformation about any other suitor who might be a threat. But since they knew of no other suitors, the wager has fallen, for the moment, on his ability to charm her."

It was the answer Alex had expected. Sir Hugh was not only known for making a nuisance of himself among his peers, but he was also a well-practised charmer of the ladies. It was something that Prinny found to be to his benefit. Sir Hugh was sure to attend any function with some pretty lady on his arm and could usually be counted on to lure along at least one or two friends of the lady with whom the prince would flirt while Sir Hugh, through sleight of hand, lined his pockets with the crown's money.

"However," Jonathan continued, "since he has seen you with her this evening, I expect he will do his best to discredit you while he charms her." He drew his horse to a stop and waited for his friend to do the same. "I must ask…"

"Yes," Alex said sharply. "Yes, she is worth the risk."

"You know he will not stop at just trying to lower you in her eyes."

Alex exhaled loudly. "I know." He circled his horse around Jonathan's. "I know that by pursuing her I will risk my position and my future plans, but frankly, neither has any meaning without her."

"You know my opinion, but I am your friend and will stand by you, which is why I did not want you to move ahead blindly."

There truly was no better friend than Jonathan Lester! A smile spread slowly across Alex's face as an idea captured his mind. "Will you also ride beside me?"

Jonathan's eyes narrowed. "I want to say yes, but I would like to know to what I am agreeing before I do so."

"It seems," Alex said lightly, "that five o'clock is a grand time to go riding in Hyde Park." He held his friend's gaze. "Tomorrow," he added in a very serious tone.

Jonathan sighed. "Must we always knock down the hive?"

"Only if we want the honey." Alex nudged his horse to move forward. "And I want the honey, Lester."

Jonathan sighed. "Very well."

Alex heard the resignation in his friend's voice. "You do not have to do this," he said. "I believe the admiral would be happy to ride with me, since it was his suggestion. If it will ease your mind, I will tell you that I do not plan to storm the castle until I am forced to do so. For now, I wish only to make my presence known."

Jonathan shook his head in disbelief. "You have already told her cousins you plan to marry her. You have sat on her step, trying to gain an audience with her, and you are using her aunt and uncle to assist you in your quest. I would say you are already well on your way to storming the castle." He chuckled. "You do typically beat down the front gate rather than waiting for it to be opened for you. You do it quietly and with few casualties, but I fear, my friend, that you are constitutionally incapable of *not* storming the castle."

Alex shrugged. He could not deny it when he looked at it from Jonathan's perspective. Though he had fallen into some fortunate circumstances, he had also quietly beaten down many doors to gain his current position.

Jonathan was still shaking his head. "I cannot believe I am about to say this, and I am not sure I will ever repeat it, so listen carefully, Madoch." He drew a deep breath. "Miss de Bourgh may actually be the best woman for you. She has a backbone; I will give you that — misdirected as it may be." He held up a hand to forestall anything Alex might have to say in reply.

"I do not want to hear it. I just want to get home to my bed. It is best to storm castles when well-rested." He clucked to his horse and was off before Alex had time to more than laugh.

"Not the best woman for me," he called after his friend, "the only one for me."

Chapter 11

ALEX PACED THE LENGTH of the green sitting room at Brownlow's townhouse. Then, he peered through the window before turning and pacing the length in the opposite direction.

"Blasted rain," he muttered for the fourteenth time in the past half hour. There would be no riding in the park and no sitting on the step at Matlock House today. And at present, he did not know where Anne would be this evening. He had hoped to discover that bit of information when he saw her at the park.

"Blasted rain." He inhaled deeply and rapidly and then exhaled just as quickly as he turned to make yet another circuit of the sitting room.

"It is not necessary to wear holes in one's boots before purchasing a new pair," Lord Rycroft said as he entered. "Brownlow will be along soon." He took a seat near the window. "I have recently been made aware of the fact that you are in town to marry my cousin." He tossed his right leg over his left knee.

Alex paused his pacing, tilted his head, and gave Anne's cousin an appraising look. How had the man come to know that information? "That is the plan if the rain ever stops." He turned toward the window at the end of the room.

"Ah, yes, rain will put a damper on outdoor plans such as riding in the park at the fashionable hour, will it not?"

Alex turned back to Rycroft, who raised a brow and steepled his fingers together in front of him while a smile curled his lips. He had definitely been talking to someone and seemed to be entertaining himself quite well by revealing bits and pieces of what he knew.

"How do you know I was planning to ride in the park?"

"My uncle."

Alex sighed in relief. At least it was not from someone who should not know.

Rycroft chuckled. "And my mother. They seem to like you. I cannot imagine there is much more that I need to know about you that my uncle has not already told me. He does not shower praise to earn friends. He only speaks highly of those he deems worthy, and it seems you are worthy." Rycroft shifted slightly in his chair. "I almost feel jealous, for I do not believe I have ever earned such accolades as you have."

Alex shook his head. "I do not know why he feels I deserve them."

"You saved his horse," Jonathan said from the corner and then turned his attention back to his book. "And you are as upstanding as any man ever was, which is one of the reasons so many of us stand with you even when we do not agree with you. You are annoyingly correct." He muttered the last bit in a tone that was very close to a growl.

"Have you met Mr. Lester?" Alex asked Rycroft.

"Not officially, but my uncle could not speak of you without speaking of him. You, Mr. Lester, also seem to hold my uncle's good opinion."

Jonathan inclined his head in acceptance. "That is Madoch's fault," he said with a smile. "As is most of the good fortune I have met in my life." He stood, placed his book on the table, and bowed. "Jonathan Lester, Mr. Madoch's man of business, at your service, my lord."

"Please." Rycroft waved the man back to his chair. "I do not stand on ceremony among friends, and since my uncle has spoken so highly of you both, I intend for us to be friends, unless there is an objection."

"You will get none from me," Alex said as he finally took a seat.

"Which means you will also get no objection from me." Jonathan picked up his book again and ignored the pointed glare that Alex was giving him. "Not that I would have objected if I had been able to form my own opinion."

"Read your book before I sack you," Alex growled.

Jonathan chuckled and opened his book. "That is not possible. I am invaluable, you know."

"Read your book," Alex growled again before turning back to Lord Rycroft. "Would you care for a game?" He motioned to the chess set at the far end of the room. "I admit to being unable to sit unoccupied for any great length of time."

"Especially when there is a plan that is being thwarted by rain," Jonathan added from behind his book.

He sighed. "Especially then."

"You remind me of my cousin Darcy." Rycroft rose from his chair, and Alex followed. "Sitting unoccupied was one thing at which I could best him. Richard and I used to challenge Darcy to a game we called observe or die. It was a bit of a dramatic name, I suppose, since no one actually died, but we were young."

Alex chuckled at the name of the game but could not fault Rycroft and his cousins for it. As a young man, he had preferred to think of his games as more daring than they likely were.

"We would pick a place to sit and an object to observe," Rycroft continued as he took a seat next to the table on which sat the chessboard and pieces. "And then, we would see who could hold their position the longest. I never won — Richard always did — but I also never lost. Darcy was always the first to quit the field, claiming he had something that needed his attention."

Rycroft arranged his pieces on the board. "However, place a book or a tiring pile of estate papers before him, and he will out-sit me every time." He chuckled. "And this is one game in which I hesitate to ever accept his challenge."

"He should play Lester."

"Good, is he?"

Alex nodded. "He can see things a few steps ahead of most people. It is part of what makes him invaluable." He smiled slowly as he placed his last piece. 'I have, however, on occasion, beaten him."

Rycroft sighed. "Are you telling me then that I have no hope?"

Alex chuckled. "My mind is a bit busy devising a plan to replace the one that has been washed away by the rain. You stand a very good chance of winning unless I can find my concentration."

Rycroft pulled a paper from his pocket. "Then I likely should not give you this as you may find it helpful in creating a new plan." He handed the note to Alex. "My mother and my wife have agreed that tonight would be an excellent night for dinner and games. Neither of them had any other soiree to attend, and, as you know, it is raining. I must warn you, however, that Anne will be there as will be the Darcys, Richard, Miss Bennet, and the Bingleys." He sighed. "Including Miss Bingley." Rycroft turned to his friend, Brownlow, who had just joined them. "Will you attend, Brownlow?"

"My sister has committed us to another dinner for this evening, and since I expect to be adding the man and his family to my own, I dare not try to alter the plans."

"Oh!" Rycroft sat up as if someone had poked him in the back. "I nearly forgot that my wife's aunt and uncle will be there and her youngest sister, who has just arrived in town to assist Kitty in wedding preparations." He rolled his eyes.

Alex gave him a puzzled look. "That seems a rather normal thing to have a sister help another sister prepare."

Rycroft chuckled. "Miss Bennet has four sisters. One of her sisters is, of course, my wife. Another is Darcy's wife, and the third is Bingley's. Miss Lydia's help is not needed, but I suspect her mother is hoping that she might be thrown in the path of some wealthy gentleman, and wedding clothes seemed as good reason as any to send her to town."

"That seems reasonable to me," Brownlow said from where he stood behind Rycroft, studying the chessboard. "I am sure if I had five daughters to see secured, I would take every opportunity available."

"She is sixteen." Rycroft moved a piece on the board.

Alex whistled softly. "That seems a trifle young to be sending her out into society."

"It is." Rycroft studied the board after Alex had made his first move. "You and Lester will come, will you not?"

Alex nodded. "Yes, and thank you."

"Good."

"I have called for tea in half an hour," Brownlow said. "Until then, I shall let you get on with your game, as I would prefer to follow Mr. Lester's lead and read."

Alex watched Brownlow stop and pick out a book from a shelf near where Lester sat. Then, he turned his eyes back to the chessboard and tried to school his mind into concentrating on the game instead of the good fortune of being able to see Anne that evening.

Two games were begun and finished within the span of time it took for tea to arrive. The first game had not gone well for Alex, but the second had seen him come very close to winning.

Rycroft let out a breath as if relieved of the possibility of a third game as the tea things were being set up.

"I am absolutely certain you would have had me at a distinct disadvantage in another round," he said while placing his pieces back on the board. "Your concentration seemed to return a quarter of the way into that second match." He chuckled. "It was also about the same time that your sole remaining knight was threatened."

Alex picked up the chess piece in question and smiled ruefully. "I do hate to see a horse endangered, and it is my belief that a king should be left with at least one noble steed when he meets his demise."

"That is the key to it," Jonathan said around a mouthful of pastry. "Threaten his knights, and he'll leave his king to save the horses. For him, it is about the horses. It is always about the horses."

He gulped down a bit of tea, seemingly unaware of the glare Alex leveled at him or the chuckles of the other gentlemen. He was not unaware of what was going on around him, of course. Jonathan was rarely oblivious to his surroundings.

"Before you begin threatening to sack me again, Madoch," he said, "I must add that that is precisely what makes you the best at what you do."

"Well said," Brownlow agreed. "I have only heard good of you."

"And that," Alex said dryly, "is another reason why I cannot sack Lester. He has an irritating way of making sure I do not ruin my reputation with a hasty decision. Like I said, he has a knack of seeing things a few steps ahead of most people."

Chapter 12

ALEX LEANED BACK IN his chair next to the small table on which the tea service was laid out and took up his cup.

"I find it difficult to believe that you would do anything in haste." Rycroft directed the statement to Alex. "You seem to be more of the calm and calculating type of gentleman rather than the rush ahead and let things fall where they may sort."

Jonathan snorted. "To a point," he agreed, "but pass that point and all bets are off, gentlemen. He would cut ties with his mother if she crossed him."

"I would not!"

"That is only because she would not cause you to ever have a need to prove me right."

"I say, you two have a very different relationship," Rycroft said. "But my uncle did mention that it was equal parts camaraderie and business."

Alex shook his head. "Truth be told, it is more friendship than business. We are nearly brothers, or, I should say, Lester is more of a brother to me than mine ever was."

"That is because we share a common interest. Your brother knows nothing about horses other than they are needed to drive his carriage and provide a means to escape the house in the morning, and, added to that, he sees your pursuit of them as only a waste of legal training."

That did sum up his brother's opinion about horses quite well and stated the main point of contention between him and his father. Alex's soft chuckle at the apt description was tinged with the bitterness that came with the strained relationship he had with the other men of his family.

"You do not lie," he agreed. "Neither he nor father was pleased when I refused to take up my robes and instead took a position with my uncle." He placed his cup on the table.

From the looks of interest on the faces of his companions, he felt his relationship with Jonathan needed some explanation. "I clerked for a year after my graduation. As was my custom in any area where I found myself, I learned who had the best horses and grooms. One of those grooms happened to have a son who was more interested in learning accounting and bookwork than in learning how to mend a harness. I traded what I knew of the subjects for the opportunity to learn what he did not wish to learn."

"He already knew how to mend a harness." Jonathan's mouth was once again full of pastry.

Alex shrugged. "True, but your father knew things that I did not, and I wanted him to share them with me." He turned toward Rycroft. "Lester's father is, in my opinion, one of the best grooms I have ever met." He smiled. "He is a man of excellence in his field, tucked away in the country, serving a country squire and as happy as any man could ever be."

"Sharing his knowledge with me," Jonathan said, "and gleaning what he could from my father kept Madoch from having to attend many social functions."

That had been quite the boon to the relationship. "I only had to attend one assembly and two or three card parties during the entirety of my term. It annoyed my employer's wife to no end, which pleased him quite well. Of course, when I did attend a soiree, I used the opportunity to meet the gentlemen of the area – that also did not please my employer's wife." He pursed his lips and thought for a moment. "I think I managed to only be required to partner one or two young ladies for a dance. They were lovely, but my heart was not available, and my plans were not to be fulfilled through courting."

"Ah, see, I was right!" Rycroft cried. "Cool and calculating."

"More like driven," Jonathan muttered.

"I find it admirable," Brownlow said. "I wish I had thought of pursuing the breeding and sale of cattle as a means to avoid social events."

Rycroft chuckled. "You are an earl, and I have never seen you at a loss for entertainment at a soiree. And, I feel as though it is my duty in my mother's stead to remind you that, unlike a second son, there is a certain level of expectation on the one to whom an inheritance and title fall."

"Do not," Brownlow grumbled, "begin speaking to me about duty, or I shall toss the lot of you out into the rain."

"It is not so bad," Rycroft said with a smile. "In fact, it can be most delightful to fulfill one's duty."

"We cannot all be so fortunate as you, Rycroft."

"Why not?" Alex looked from one gentleman to the other. Brownlow's was an attitude that had long bothered him. "I see no reason why every man, titled or not, cannot find happiness in marriage. It does not need to be a matter of chance."

"The strictures of society prevent it," Brownlow answered. "It is nearly impossible to get to know a lady. She is told how to speak, what to say, what not to say, how to laugh and bat her eyelashes. It is nothing more than a show. They are all actresses, but their stage is not in a theater: it is in a ballroom or a drawing room."

Alex tipped his head to the side as he considered what Brownlow had said, but he could not – would not – accept it. There had to be a way. "Perhaps you are not looking in the proper places then. It cannot be as hopeless as that."

"You must excuse my friend's opinions, for he still does not attend functions to spend time with ladies," Jonathan inserted before turning his attention to Alex. "I assure you, Madoch, that what Brownlow says is true. You should pay more attention to these things."

"Then I do not see why it must continue in such a fashion." He shook his head. "What gain can there be in being tied to someone whom you deceived into accepting you?"

Jonathan sighed as if they had had this conversation before, which they had, and it was bound to be one they would have again since Lester seemed unwilling to admit that society could and should change.

"It is not a deception," he said. "It is showing oneself to best advantage."

"Presenting perfection is deception," Alex countered. "There is not one person living or dead, save the good Lord himself, who is perfect. Why must one pretend to be such? It will surely only bring disappointment and embarrassment when the truth is discovered. It is much better to simply be yourself." He scowled. "Unless, of course, yourself is entirely unacceptable. Then one might try a bath and some lessons in etiquette," he held up a cautioning finger, "not acting."

A small growl emanated from Jonathan, and Alex could see the storm clouds brewing in his friend's demeanour. It would blow through quickly. He would make his point. Alex would counter it, and then, all would be well. Therefore, he paid no mind to the noise of displeasure and selected a sweet treat from the tray.

"Then, my friend," Jonathan said in a flat but serious tone, "why do you insist on concealing your true value and connections? Are you not lying to try to win Miss de Bourgh's hand?"

"No, I am not."

"How are you not?" Rycroft asked.

"Concealing would mean I am covering up a truth. I am not." A small amount of guilt had begun to form in Alex's mind. It did seem to be a bit less noble now that he heard himself defend it.

"A sin of omission is still a sin," muttered Jonathan.

Alex paused, taking as long as possible to chew the morsel of cake he had just popped into his mouth. Perhaps his friend was correct. Perhaps he was being just as deceitful as the many misses who stood in the ballroom saying only what they were allowed and never straying from the prescribed form of behaviour. He swallowed and took a sip of tea to rinse the stickiness from his palate.

"Not presenting her with my circumstances is necessary," he said.

"So you admit I am right." Jonathan had crossed his arms and was glaring at his friend.

"I maintain that I am concealing nothing." Alex straightened a sleeve. "I am merely not revealing all — and for very good reason. I must know the truth of her heart, and if she knows all, that truth will be clouded."

"How do you suppose she will respond when she discovers that you have not been open with her about your standing?"

She would likely bluster. Alex let out a frustrated breath. Perhaps his plan was not as good as he had thought it was. "Miss de Bourgh has already discounted my success as an impossibility. She would not believe me if I told her."

"Then show her," suggested Jonathan. "Take her to St. James's."

"No!" His frustration pushed him to his feet. "That place is not fit for a proper lady — at least it has not seemed to be when I have been there." He paced the length of the room and returned. "And then, how would I know if she chose me for me and not for my connections?" That issue still remained. "Perhaps I should cut my ties to the place. Then there would be nothing to omit. I would be as she declared me." He scrubbed his face with his hands.

"Perhaps the rain will clear," commented Brownlow causing all eyes to turn toward him. "If the rain clears, then you could go for a ride. Nothing clears the mind more than a lonely jaunt on a horse."

"Not always," Rycroft said before turning the conversation back to the topic. "If you cut ties from His Highness, what will become of you? What do you have to offer my cousin?" He smiled and softened his tone. "Aside from your heart, of course."

Alex drew a breath. "I have a small estate left to me by a distant relation. An entailment," he explained. "It is near Brighton, and I travel to it regularly, but my main residence to this point has been a small house in Brighton. I see no need to rattle around an estate except when needed to see that improvements are begun to aid in the raising of horses... some fence repairs, a new stable, some slight alterations in the planting of crops, that sort of thing."

"And you would take that as your primary residence and livelihood?"

Alex nodded. "I have set aside a substantial sum for future living and would still offer my services in assisting gentlemen to find horses to meet their needs, even if they are not my horses." He smiled at Rycroft's chuckle.

"It is a well-thought-out plan," said Brownlow, "except for one thing. Will you be able to sever your ties to the school at Brighton?"

"Perhaps not completely."

"But we have considered that," Jonathan said with a smile. "We entered the agreement with the prince knowing that, eventually, we might need an escape."

Alex clapped his friend on the shoulder. "As I said, gentlemen, Lester here sees several steps ahead, which makes him invaluable."

The men spent several more moments in conversation regarding horses and plans, hearts and ladies before Brownlow moved to break up the group by citing a need to prepare to accompany his sister to her dinner party.

"I dare say my wife will be wondering what has become of me." Rycroft stood. "Although," he said with a smile, "a few more minutes might earn me a scolding. Perhaps I shall stay."

Brownlow shook his head. "You are incorrigible," he called as he left the room.

"I am not staying," Rycroft called after him. He moved toward the door and then turned back. "Do not tell Anne. Arrange your life as if she has accepted you. Present your financial papers to her if you wish, but do not tell her about your connections. If she discovers them, so be it." He looked levelly at both gentlemen. "I agree with Madoch. Marriage should be based on mutual affection. Do not settle for less." He gave them each a bow of his head and then left.

"Will you present your papers?" Jonathan asked.

"Not yet. If I knew beyond a doubt that she still harboured feelings for me – which I think she does – then I might. I do not wish to live my life wondering if she loved me or my money. I am sorry. I know it is not what you wish to hear, but I have seen one marriage too many where wealth was the only thing that both the husband and wife liked about each other." His had not been an unhappy home when he was growing up, but his parents' strained relationship was not the ideal he sought.

"Shall I write his majesty a letter stating a desire to meet?" Jonathan asked as they climbed the stairs to their guest rooms.

Alex nodded. "It will take time." Gaining an audience with the prince was not easy, although, for those on whom he relied for advice and who were directly involved with his ventures such as the riding school, as Alex was, it was not quite so difficult. Still, his majesty moved only when his majesty deemed it to be suitable.

"Have you ever wondered," Jonathan said as he stood outside his room, "why Miss de Bourgh insists on wealth and position?"

"What do you mean?"

"I know why you insist on a love match and why wealth has been of little value to you beyond seeing that it is accumulated to provide for a family. Your father and mother's marriage is not one for which you wish." He shrugged as he opened the door. "Could it be possible that she has a similar reason?" He stepped into his room and, closing the door, left a gaping Alex standing in the hall, pondering his words.

Chapter 13

WHILE ALEX WAS PACING the drawing room at Lord Brownlow's home, Anne was once again discovering that what she *thought* she wanted was not, in fact, what she wanted.

Since the drawing room was currently free of visitors who were there to see her, she excused herself and took herself down the hall and into the library. Closing the door, she leaned against it and expelled a frustrated breath. There had been half a dozen callers today, and, on paper, all of them appeared to be exactly what she sought. However, just as on the previous day, this set of gentlemen was as exciting as a long and wordy sermon by her mother's parson, and that was not what she wished to endure every day for the rest of her life.

She pushed off the door and ran her fingers along the backs of chairs and tops of tables as she made a circuit of the room. Then, she stood in the middle of library and turned a complete circle. This is what she wanted. A life designed as elegantly as this room and filled with fine things and tales of adventure, nothing extraordinary, but small trips, little visits, friends whose very presence filled you with joy. This room felt safe. This room felt full.

The drawing room, on the other hand, though filled with people, had felt empty, and her footing in there had felt as if she were walking on the top rail of a narrow fence – one wrong step and she would plummet into some sort of injury. Every potential suitor who had called since she had placed that ad in the paper were qualified. They had titles. They had wealth. And not all of them were insupportably lacking in countenance or carriage, though a few were rather wanting in one or both areas.

She shook her head. Why, if they were acceptable, did she feel as if they were not? It was most vexing! How was she to choose a suitable husband?

She was so caught up in her contemplations that she jumped at the sound of a soft knock. She turned toward the sound just as the door opened slowly.

"I apologize for disrupting your solitude, Miss de Bourgh." Sir Hugh stepped into the room and left the door slightly ajar but nearly closed. "I saw you go into this room as I entered, and I was afraid you were distressed. Are you well?" He crossed the room and came to stand near her.

"I am. I just needed a few minutes to think." She smiled at him as if her troublesome thoughts had not just turned to consider how his arrival had disturbed the tranquility of the room and to wonder if it was just because he had entered and spoken or if it was something more. "It is a grey and dreary day, is it not?"

"I was sorry to see the rain," he said. "I am afraid our drive will have to be postponed. That is what I came to tell you." He took a step closer. "I was also rather hopeful that in place of our drive, you would allow me to spend a few moments with you doing something – perhaps reading or playing the piano?"

"Do you play?" That would be lovely if he did. She loved to listen to an accomplished pianist whenever she could.

Sir Hugh blinked. "No... well... yes, but just a bit," he stammered.

Well, that was disappointing.

"Then you are far more accomplished than I," she admitted while fixing her eyes on one of the flowers that decorated the rug on which they stood. "I attempted to learn, but to no avail. Playing is not my talent." She glanced up at him and then returned her eyes to the flower. Somehow speaking to a flower was much easier than speaking to the handsome man beside her.

"While I do not play, I can sing. However, I do not perform." She flinched as he placed a hand on her arm and then slid it down to grasp her hand. Not because it was unpleasant. It was not. It was startling.

"I apologize if my desire to spend time with you has made you feel uneasy," he said as he led her to a settee near the window. "It was not my intent, and I do hope you will not fault me for it. I am willing to do whatever you choose."

"Why?" Anne arranged her skirts about her as she took a seat. She found her tingling fingers and fluttering tummy to be unsettling, and so before they could disconcert her any longer, she chose to redirect the conversation and keep her hands safely out of his.

"What do you mean?" He was blinking at her in a startled fashion once again.

"I do not like to play games, Sir Hugh," she said softly. "I find it best to be as direct in my dealings as is acceptable."

She tipped her head to the side, furrowed her brows, and pursed her lips for a moment before adding, "Although I seem to not always know where acceptable ends and forward begins."

It was a dreadful thing to be so. It had not been while at Rosings, but here, in town, it did seem to be a rather unhelpful trait. She shook herself slightly from her contemplation of that and continued with what she had intended to tell him.

"I see no reason to make this ordeal anything more than it has to be. I have advertised for a husband. I do not expect a love match, but rather a pleasant business arrangement. I shall serve as hostess and attend to all the duties expected of a wife while my husband will tend to his duty of providing securely for myself and any children. A friendship would be desirable, of course, but I am under no illusion that one must swoon with admiration in the presence of her spouse to have a comfortable and pleasant life."

She folded her hands in her lap as her heart whispered that a marriage could be more, and a fleeting image of Alex passed through her mind. She pushed them both away. That was not a match that was meant to be. It would be unwise. She must focus on the reality of her situation and making as wise a choice as she possibly could. The safety and security of her future depended upon it.

"My desire," she continued, "is not to hear pretty words but to become familiar with you to see if we would suit. You need not pretend to be enamoured of me."

He was blinking at her again. "I do not pretend," he finally said. "I find you pleasing to the eye, and your forthrightness, while I must admit it takes me by surprise, is quite refreshing." His eyes swept over her figure. "Very pleasing," he said with a smile. "It would not be a hardship to fulfill my duties as your husband," he muttered just loudly enough for her to hear as he took her hand once again.

If he had expected her to blush, he was not to be disappointed. How could she not blush? He was being quite improper! However, if he had expected her to quietly turn the conversation, he was to be startled once again. There were things she needed to know.

"You mentioned before that you would not take a mistress after you were married unless it became necessary." Despite the heat flooding her face and the rapid beating of her heart from the anxiety she felt at discussing such an indelicate topic, Anne continued, "I assume that it will become necessary should you find me not satisfying?"

He cleared his throat. It was obviously not what he had expected her to say. "I meant if my wife turned me away."

Her brows furrowed. Having wrested as much information as possible from her governess, a young, widowed woman who found it necessary to support herself, Anne knew about what happened between a man and a woman once married. "But a wife must turn her husband away at times when she is incapable of receiving his attentions."

"I did not speak of indisposition but of refusal when no need for such exists."

She nodded. The words of Mr. Blackmoore on the balcony about how many men kept mistresses still played in her mind. She did not wish for a husband who would take a mistress after they were married, nor did she wish to be betrothed to a man who currently had one. "One more question, and then we shall put this improper topic away. Do you have a mistress now?"

"I do not see how that affects the discussion of our marrying. Whether I do or do not have a mistress now, I shall not once I marry."

She pulled her hand from his. "Then, you do have one?"

"I did not say I did," he retorted.

"Nor," she shot back, "did you say you did not. Therefore, I will assume you do."

She rose to her feet. She knew she should dismiss him as she had Blackmoore, but there was part of her that still wished to see him. It was wrong, she supposed, to allow him to remain merely because he was attractive, but she would give the rightness or wrongness of her decision to allow him to stay more consideration later. For now, she was going to take the opportunity to spend some time with a gentleman doing something other than reviewing financial papers and listening to family histories.

"I must say it is a mark against you," she said, turning to look at him. "Not that you have a mistress, per se – although I do not condone it, of course – but because you attempted to conceal the fact. Deceit is a far more grievous sin." Her heart pricked at the thought of his perfidy. She should not trust him, it seemed to say, but instead of paying heed to its whispering, she took a breath and smiled at Sir Hugh.

"You are not to be discarded for one error, so if you wish to spend an hour with me once my other guests have left, I prefer poetry about nature to the sonnets of Shakespeare. I am certain you will find something suitable on the shelves of this room. Until then, Sir Hugh." She dipped a curtsey and turned to leave, but he caught her hand and, rising, pulled her into his embrace and kissed her quite soundly.

"In case I am dismissed for some other error, I did not wish to leave without a taste of your sweet lips," he explained before kissing her once again. "Delicious," he whispered as he broke the kiss but not his hold on her.

Anne felt as if her legs were about to fail her. Shock and pleasure fought for dominance in her mind. She willed her arms to push away from him, but they would not listen. And so, she remained wrapped in his delightful embrace until a gasp – a familiar, criticizing gasp – caused her formerly unwilling body to move quite forcefully and rapidly away from Sir Hugh.

"Anne!" Her mother stood for a moment looking at her and, then with another less displeased gasp and a small smile, she turned toward the hall and called for her sister and brother.

"Mother!" Anne took Lady Catherine by the arm and attempted to pull her into the library. "It is not necessary to call for my aunt and uncle."

"Is it not?" Lady Catherine fairly sang the question. Looking into the room, she added, "He is an excellent gentleman. So handsome. It was very clever of you to arrange a compromise. Wishing to see me, indeed! I should have known you would never call me for some trivial thing."

Anne was certain her heart had dropped to her toes. "Call you?"

"Yes, yes, Harrison said you wished to see me."

"I never called you." Anne gripped her mother's arm more tightly and once again attempted to pull her into the library. Why would Harrison lie to her mother like that?

"Oh, but you did, and you had left in such a haste that I assumed you were unwell. However, I could not get away from my guests quite as quickly as I would have liked, but then, it seems I was just in time." She looked around Anne to Sir Hugh and sighed happily. "Such a fine-looking son I shall have. You are such a clever girl."

Chapter 14

ANNE'S MOUTH HUNG OPEN as she stared at her babbling, excited mother. This could not be happening. Surely, her mother was not going to force her to marry Sir Hugh, was she?

"I assure you, Mother, that I did not send for you. I was not unwell. I just needed a few moments of quiet and then, Sir Hugh arrived..." Her eyes grew wide, and her thought hung unfinished as she began to grasp what had actually happened. The cad had planned this!

"Yes, he did, did he not?" Lady Catherine's voice was nearly gleeful. "Such a clever girl," she said. "Sophia, Anne is to marry Sir Hugh."

Anne shook her head. "No. I am not!"

"Oh, but why else would you be kissing him?"

"Mother, please," Anne said. "Keep your voice down. Do you wish for everyone to know?" She tugged again on her mother's arm and this time, with the help of her aunt, managed to guide Lady Catherine into the library.

Admiral Fitzwilliam closed the door as Lady Catherine was being seated. "What has you bellowing in such an unladylike fashion, Catherine?" His voice was nearly as severe as the glare he directed at Sir Hugh, who nervously straightened his jacket. "Anne will be marrying no one unless she has my approval."

"You must give it," Lady Catherine said. "He has kissed her, and so he must marry her."

"Do you wish to marry Sir Hugh?" The admiral turned his ferocious gaze from Sir Hugh and directed it more softly at his niece.

"I had thought I might, but no." She shook her head slowly. "No, I do not. He planned this." Her voice wavered as she tried to contain her emotions. How dare he do this to her? How dare he attempt to take her choice from her?

"There you have it, Catherine," the admiral said. "Anne shall not be marrying Sir Hugh."

"But she must!" Lady Catherine cried. "Think of the scandal if she does not."

"How will there be a scandal?" Lady Sophia asked. "No one knows of this outside of this room."

"And they shall never know of it," added the admiral.

Anne shivered slightly at the danger contained in the tone of her uncle's warning, and yet no matter how foreboding his tone, it was comforting. He wished to know her desires and would see that they were fulfilled if he could.

Sir Hugh must have heard the warning, as well, because he lowered his eyes and mumbled his agreement.

Lady Catherine, however, seemed impervious to the tone. Either that or she was just unwilling to comply. Whichever it was, she was not through attempting to see her daughter married. "The door was open. There are servants, and we had guests. It is possible that the tale will be spread, and one cannot control how it might alter in the telling."

"I will not allow the marriage, and Anne cannot marry without my approval. That is the end of it," the admiral said. "Added to that, Anne has not accepted any offer, and as far as I know, none was made. Whatever tale we might encounter must be refuted as a lie." He turned to Sir Hugh. "I suspect your welcome as a suitor has run its course. We shall remain cordial unless you insist it be otherwise. Any unwanted advances toward my niece or whispers about her will be counted as an insistence."

Anne watched the way Sir Hugh's mouth tightened, and his eyes narrowed just a bit before he nodded, gave his agreement, and took his leave.

Lady Catherine threw her hands up in the air. "I begin to wonder if you will ever marry. First, you refuse your cousin and make a spectacle of yourself with an announcement. Now, you allow a gentleman liberties and refuse his suit!" She huffed and flopped back in her seat. "There will not be a proper gentleman in all England who will consider you if you continue as you have."

"Catherine," Admiral Fitzwilliam growled. "Your daughter has taken an unconventional route to finding a husband, but she has done nothing wrong in refusing a man such as Sir Hugh."

"Nothing wrong?" Lady Catherine harrumphed. "He seemed a proper gentleman."

"*Seemed*, I believe, is the correct word," Lady Sophia said softly. "Not all who appear to be proper are." She placed a comforting arm around Anne's shoulders. "It is a disappointment when the truth is discovered; however, we were fortunate to learn of it before connections could not be reversed."

"I would like to go to my room." Anne's head was beginning to throb, and her chest felt tight and painful.

"A rest might help," Lady Sophia agreed. "You are expected at dinner at Rycroft Place this evening. You would not wish to disappoint Lady Rycroft." Her lips curled into a smile as they always did as she said the title.

Anne knew how happy her aunt was to have added Mary to her family. Anne also knew how happy Mary and her cousin were. She attempted to smile in return, but the tightness of her chest kept her from succeeding.

"I will accompany you," Lady Sophia said. "Reginald, please have a bit of something sent up, and Catherine, inform Harrison that Anne is not home to any other callers today."

She paused for a moment before giving her sister a pointed look. "If you love your daughter at all, you will not speak about what happened here with anyone."

"If I love my daughter!" Catherine harumphed. "Of course, I love my daughter."

"Then, you will want what is best for her," the admiral said as he offered her his arm. "Just as we all do," he added with an encouraging smile for Anne before escorting her mother from the room.

Anne followed her uncle and mother from the room and started on her way to her room with Lady Sophia. Her limbs felt as heavy as her heart did.

"Are you well?" her aunt asked as they took the stairs side by side.

Anne nodded and then gave a small shrug. How was one supposed to feel when one had been tricked? Part of her wished to run after Sir Hugh and make him explain why he had done what he had done, while another part longed to forget all that had just happened, climb under her covers on her bed, and begin the day again.

"You are an attractive match," her aunt said as if she knew what Anne had been thinking. "You have both wealth and connections, as well as beauty." She opened the door to Anne's room and entered.

Anne crossed to the window and looked down at the wet street. She saw people moving quickly from house to carriage and servants scurrying on their errands with collars pulled high and hats pulled down against the weather.

"I stood here this morning," she said, not turning from the scene, "and I was upset because I would not be able to go for a drive. I have never been on a drive with a gentleman, you know." She sat on the cushion in the window seat and kicked off her shoes. She pulled her feet up under her skirts but remained positioned in such a way that she could still watch the people below.

"If he had attempted a compromise in public, I would have been forced to marry him." She drew a shaking breath. "I would have found myself precisely where I did not wish to be, unable to do as I wanted because someone had more power than I did." She rested her head against the wall at her back. Weariness pressed down upon her. "How does one remain safe?" Would she always feel as if she was struggling to be seen and heard? Was that just how her life was supposed to be?

Lady Sophia joined Anne at the window. "Safety is never guaranteed."

Anne sighed. "Then, how am I to choose?"

"What did your heart tell you about Sir Hugh? Did it feel safe when in his presence, or was it excited or maybe unsure?"

Anne considered the question and thought of how her heart had told her to dismiss Sir Hugh, but her mind had overruled her heart. If she had but listened. She shook her head at her own foolishness.

"It was unsure. I liked his attention and found him handsome, but I never felt at ease. I thought I might learn to feel so. After all, I had only met him and knew very little about him."

Lady Sophia patted Anne's knee. "Just so. Your heart is an excellent guide if you will listen to it carefully. It is not above being tricked, but there will often be that little worry, hanging at the back of your mind, when your heart desires something it should not. Let it guide you, and then ask for advice. I will always tell you the truth. You know that, do you not?"

"I do." Anne gave her aunt a small smile and then turned her attention to the scene outside her window. There was only one gentleman who had ever made her feel safe, but he was not a wise choice because he had neither wealth nor position enough to not be constantly swayed to do what he might not wish to do by someone like her mother or her uncle, Lord Matlock. If only she could marry where her heart wished. She sighed and attempted to turn her mind away from comparing Sir Hugh and Alex.

However, her thoughts and the silence which reigned in the room were unbroken until a tray containing two small glasses of sherry and a few biscuits arrived.

"Marrying for love alone is not enough," Anne said as she took a sip of sherry and wrinkled her nose. It was not her favourite drink.

"And I believe, unlike your mother or Lady Matlock, that marrying for position alone is also not enough," her aunt countered. "Matrimony is a tricky business."

"It is indeed." Anne ate a biscuit in silence and finished her drink. If there were truly no way to be safe in marriage, then, why marry? Perhaps that was her answer.

"Marriage is not for everyone," she said more to herself than her aunt. "I did not want to always live in my mother's house." She shrugged. "I had hoped to have a home of my own to run, but perhaps it is not to be. Maybe I should return to Rosings and find some work to occupy my time – a charity perhaps?"

Lady Sophia placed her empty glass on the tray and then crossed to Anne and kissed her forehead. "You need a rest. I do not believe you are destined to remain unwed." She cupped her niece's chin and lifted it so that Anne looked up at her. "Let your heart choose," she said gently. "Promise me you will give it a bit more time before returning to Rosings? I would miss you dearly if you left too soon."

Anne could not help but smile. Was it possible to exchange her mother for her aunt? She loved how loved she felt when with Lady Sophia.

"I will not return to Rosings until after I have visited Hertfordshire and have shared in the celebration of my cousin Richard's wedding. However, if I have not found a prospect by then, I shall go home with my mother."

Lady Sophia kissed her on the forehead once again. "You are not giving me very long to help you, but I will do my best." She turned to leave. "Do you wish to sort the papers from today's visit after your rest?"

"Have them placed in my sitting room," Anne replied with a nod.

"Very well. I shall see you at dinner?" There was a slight lift of uncertainty in her voice.

"You will," Anne assured.

"Rest well." Sophia closed the door softly.

Anne climbed onto her bed. She knew it would be more comfortable to undress, but she did not wish to call for her maid. She wished to lie here in her tangled mess of emotions alone and dismiss them in sleep. To that end, she closed her eyes and drew a deep breath of the peaceful, soundless air and released it slowly and repeatedly until, finally, her mind drifted away from the worries of the day and into the land of dreams.

Chapter 15

ANNE TURNED TO THE right and then the left as she stood in front of the mirror. She pulled her shoulders up and back and looked again from side to side. Satisfied with what she saw, she dismissed her maid.

She stood for a few more moments where she was and ran a finger along the gold chain of her necklace as she thought. Her sleep had been refreshing to her body and partially to her mind. The removal of one man, no matter how handsome or charming he might have been, did not mean her search was at an end. There were many more names on papers in the sitting room. Surely one of them might prove to be an appropriate – even wise – choice. It might even be possible for her to speak to her uncle and have the most promising candidates investigated. That way, she could know more about them than what they presented.

"It is a good plan," she said aloud before giving her reflection a nod and turning to leave the room.

That lingering feeling of never being truly safe hung at the edges of her mind as she descended the stairs which she had only hours ago climbed in search of refuge from events that had transpired in the library.

She drew a long breath – one which took two whole steps down the stairs to complete – and instructed herself that with her exhale, she would push all thoughts of duplicitous men from her mind.

"You look lovely." Admiral Fitzwilliam greeted her at the bottom of the stairs with a smile.

"Thank you."

His smile faded. "Your mother has asked to see you before you go, but I have not given her my word that you would. The choice is entirely up to you."

She sighed and considered not seeing her mother, but then, she knew if she did not at least make a brief appearance, her mother would comment on it for days, if not weeks. Sometimes, when it was not too taxing to do so, it was best to just appease Lady Catherine, and Anne knew this was one of those times. "I will say a quick farewell."

And she did. After a few moments of conversation with her mother and Lord and Lady Matlock, Anne was back at her uncle's side and being handed into the carriage.

"Are you looking forward to the celebration?" he asked as she settled into her seat, and he took his. "Sophia mentioned that a special cake has been commissioned for Miss Katherine, although, I am told, it is to be a surprise to her from her sisters. So, we mustn't let on that we know."

Anne wondered what it would be like to have a family of siblings who planned special treats for one another to mark momentous occasions such as a betrothal.

"And Rycroft has invited several friends," her uncle continued, "so that games can be played, and I know that if he has his way, a dance or two will be had. All in all, it promises to be a delightful evening."

Her uncle chuckled. "I still find it amazing that two such opposite people as Rycroft and his lady should make such a good match. That boy could try the nerves of a saint."

"Then perhaps she is an angel and not a saint?" Anne, too, had noticed how very different in personalities Lord and Lady Rycroft were, but it did not seem to hinder their relationship. In fact, it seemed that it aided it as one complemented the other perfectly. "I am quite anxious to see Lady Rycroft as well as Mrs. Darcy and Miss Katherine."

"Lady Rycroft? Mrs. Darcy? Miss Katherine?" Her uncle's tone was one of surprise. "I thought you called them by their Christian names? I have not missed some important development, have I?"

"No, you have missed nothing. It is just that it is a formal event," she explained. "Besides, I believe you led the conversation by referring to them formally."

He chuckled. "So I did. I suppose it is as you said, the thought of it being a special occasion which is at fault. It is not every day that one gets to celebrate a betrothal of a nephew to a lady as lovely as Kitty." He shifted in his seat. "It is sad that Richard's parents could not attend, but Sophia agreed that it might be best to keep it to the younger set and a couple of old chaperones."

The light was not great in the carriage, but Anne was positive that the comment had been made with a wink.

"I am quite pleased for Richard. He has found a fine wife." Kitty was all that was sweet and good. Theirs would be a happy marriage where neither would put anyone or anything in a position of power over the other. That was what she wanted. What she longed for with every fibre of her being.

"Finally, we Fitzwilliams will have a family that is happy instead of one made up of the fighting factions of my generation and the one which came before." He sighed. "Lord Matlock has done his best to keep things as they were, but thanks to you and your cousins, his ways have been tumbled for a time."

He reached across the carriage and patted her knee. "You do know that my greatest wish for you is that you are just as happy, do you not?"

"I do," she said in a voice that was just above a whisper.

"Then I must express my opinion on a matter." He shifted again in his seat, this time leaning towards her and grasping her hands. "I lost my love a long time ago. I have tried on many occasions to find something, anything, that would fill the void left by her absence. The sea came close, but that is now gone, and the empty place remains." He chuckled wryly. "We remain friends, but she has established her life and seems content, for that I cannot help but be happy."

"Did she marry?" Anne bit her lip after the question left her mouth. She hoped he would not be offended by her curiosity.

He squeezed her hands. "She did. I wish with all that I am that I would have followed my heart. Trust me when I say that there is no greater regret than to have been so close to grasping happiness and having it slip away, never to return. I beg you to consider my error before you make any choice about marriage. Please. Please, promise me this."

There was no mistaking the urgency in her uncle's voice. She could only imagine the grief that lay behind it. She pressed her lips together as the distant memory of searing pain at knowing she had to send her heart's choice away flitted through her mind.

She nodded. "I will consider it." But it would not change what could not be. It could not change it, could it?

"Thank you. I would not be doing my duty to you if I did not ask you to ponder such things, since I know intimately how great the weight of choosing wrongly can be," he said as the carriage drew to a stop in front of Rycroft House.

Again, Anne nodded. What else could she do? Was there anything that she could say to bring comfort other than her promise to do as he had asked?

⁂

Mary stood between Rycroft and Kitty, waiting to greet Anne. "I am so happy to see you, Anne. I have been longing for a visit from you, but Lady Sophia tells me you have been very busy with interviews."

"I most certainly have been!" Anne leaned close to Mary and lowered her voice. "However, it has not been enjoyable. All my callers are rather dull, and I would much rather spend time with you and your sisters."

Mary smiled and pulled Anne into an embrace. "Tomorrow, you must join us at the museum."

"I would like that." Anne felt a sigh of relief pass through her at the thought of not having to be subjected to yet another round of uninteresting interviews.

"You have not yet met our sister, Lydia," Kitty said as she took Anne's hand and gave it a gentle squeeze. "I can assure you that our visit will be anything but dull with her along."

Mary chuckled. "She has improved in the last month, but she is still Lydia."

A rather loud giggle was heard from the drawing room.

"That is Lydia," Mary said. "She is rarely quiet. Come."

She wrapped her arm around Anne's, ignoring the look of displeasure from her husband at being displaced by his cousin. That action made Anne laugh softly.

"I will introduce you," Mary said as they moved down the entrance hall. "Everyone else is here, so we are just beginning with some wine in the drawing room while we wait for our meal to be ready."

"Georgiana was allowed to come." Kitty had taken Anne's other arm. "Since we did not wish the men to outnumber the ladies."

"Samuel invited some friends." There was a hint of concern in Mary's voice.

"Yes, my uncle mentioned he had."

"Did he mention names?" Mary asked.

Anne shook her head.

Mary sighed. "There was one whom Samuel did not wish to invite, but things have changed, and it really could not be helped."

Anne stopped walking. They were just outside the door to the drawing room, and she could clearly hear Alex's voice. Alex was counted among her cousin's friends?

"And who might these guests be?" she asked, turning toward Rycroft.

Rycroft glanced at Richard and the admiral as if asking for their support. "Madoch, Lester, Endicott, and Blackmoore." He grimaced at the last name. "He is the one that could not be helped. Please stay."

"All will be well," Mary assured her. "Mr. Blackmoore has offered for Miss Bingley and has been accepted. He has also apologized to Samuel and promises to be on his best behaviour. He knows that his footing is tenuous. Should he be dismissed from this gathering, he might also lose Miss Bingley."

She leaned her head closer to Anne's and lowered her voice. "Mr. Bingley and Mr. Hurst were not pleased to hear of the cut he received, and, were they not so anxious to rid themselves of their sister, I doubt his offer would have found success. However, it has, and we, therefore, must extend a tentative welcome whether we wish to or not."

"My wife is of the *not* ranks," Rycroft whispered.

Anne smiled at that but shook her head. Her body wished to run from the house, but her stubborn nature would not allow it. She also knew that she would place a cloud of disappointment over the party if she did not stay, and so she would. That did not mean she would do so without making her displeasure at the circumstances known. She would not dance around disquieting circumstances again today. She had done that once in the library and that had almost ended in disaster.

"I have had my fill of trying gentlemen today," she said as she glared at Rycroft. "I will stay, but if either Mr. Blackmoore or Mr. Madoch do anything to make me uneasy, I will leave."

"No," her cousin replied firmly, "they will leave. Not you. I promise. I have told Blackmoore as much, and as Mary said, he has given his word, although I am not certain I put much faith in it."

"All will be well," Mary tried to assure once again.

Anne wanted to believe her.

"Rycroft has a pistol, and I am a crack shot," the admiral whispered, causing Anne and the others to laugh. "So, you see, you truly have nothing to fear."

Anne shook her head again and drew a deep breath. "Very well, I shall stay as long as Rycroft's pistols are handy."

Mary tightened her arm around Anne's and gave her one more reassuring smile before they entered the room.

Anne, hoping that she was doing a credible job of looking the part of a self-assured lady, smiled and curtseyed in greeting to all who were gathered. Thankfully, everyone returned to their prior conversations as soon as introductions had been made, and Anne found a seat next to Kitty and tucked out of view of the two gentlemen whom she wished to avoid. There, she occupied herself by observing the occupants of the room and attending half-heartedly to the conversation between Kitty and Elizabeth until dinner was announced.

Chapter 16

FINALLY, AFTER WHAT FELT like an interminable amount of time but was likely no more than a quarter of an hour, dinner was announced, and Anne put her thoughts about troubling men and her future away.

"Oh, la!"

Anne barely refrained from grimacing at Miss Lydia's exclamation of delight.

"Who shall escort me to dinner?" Miss Lydia looked hopefully around the room.

Next to Anne, Kitty groaned, and Elizabeth closed her eyes while Mary, who stood next to Rycroft, gave her youngest sister a decidedly pointed look.

"Please do not subject me to taking her into dinner," Alex begged from behind Anne. "I would much rather converse with a friend."

Anne turned towards him.

"Please."

"Of course." She had opened her mouth to refuse, but when he smiled at her just then, she found her words turning to those of acceptance instead of refusal.

"Thank you." Alex extended his arm to her.

Anne hesitated before taking it. It was required that she take his arm, but she knew that doing so would only make her heart yearn for him more than it already did. "This is only as friends," she reminded herself and him.

He nodded his agreement, but there was something about his eyes that made Anne believe he was not being entirely truthful with her.

"We will sit by one of your cousins, and you shall be perfectly safe," he said.

She began to smile at him in acceptance of his proclamation, for that was what she was sure was expected, but then thought better of it. Since when, she chided herself, had she done something simply because it was expected rather than stating her mind on a subject? "I fear you are not being truthful," she said as they walked.

He shook his head. "I am afraid you are wrong. I have no intentions of placing you in the way of danger."

"Perhaps," she agreed as she took her seat, "but you do not intend for us to be mere friends."

"For this meal, I do." He smiled at her and flicked an eyebrow. "Beyond this evening, you know my wish."

"It shall not be granted."

"That remains to be seen," he replied. "Now, shall we turn the topic before you become distressed, and I am ousted from the house? My stomach has been rumbling for half an hour, and I have no intention of going hungry."

"Very well," she conceded. "Of what do you wish to speak? Your uncle?"

He smiled fondly as he had always done when thinking about his uncle. "My uncle is well, though he has a bit of gout in his foot, which slows him, but his business is thriving. There is nary a soul who is not pleased with his service. After all, his stable boasts nearly the finest horses in Brighton."

She laughed. "If you are trying to sell me on his business, Mr. Madoch, you should be saying that his horses are the finest, not nearly the finest."

He smiled. "Ah, but that I cannot do."

"No," said his friend who was seated next to him. "His Highness would not be best pleased to hear his are not the finest." He lowered his voice to just above a whisper before adding, "Even if they are outshone by Madoch's uncle."

"You remember Mr. Lester, do you not?" Alex asked Anne. "I believe you met him once before."

"I am not certain if I do remember him." Anne studied Mr. Lester's face for a moment. He did look oddly familiar, but she could not place him.

"We went riding six years ago – you, me, and Madoch," Jonathan tipped his head and looked back at her. "I believe it was the day before Madoch and I departed for Brighton."

"That was you?" she asked softly. Her mind recalled him perfectly now. She had slipped from her room to meet Alex for a ride and had found him in the company of a friend.

"It was."

"Forgive me for my lack of memory," she apologized.

"It is understandable. It has been six years, and ours was but a passing acquaintance." Mr. Lester's eyes moved from her face to his plate. "I've not had the opportunity to forget you," he said softly.

She heard the accusation in Mr. Lester's tone and looked at Alex, who shrugged. "I often speak of home, and since you are part of those memories, I fear Lester has heard of you often."

Anne attempted a small smile that she did not feel as she focused on the vegetables on her plate. Such comments were definitely not keeping her safe, no matter how closely she sat to any of her cousins or their wives.

He had spoken of her and thought of her – often. She wondered if it had been as often as she had thought of him and if he had thought of her in a flattering way or a vengeful way. That thought startled her. Perhaps he wished to marry her, not because he still loved her, but because he wished to repay her for shunning him. Perhaps he did not want to marry her at all. Perhaps he wished for her to want to marry him, so that he could toss her aside.

She stabbed a carrot particularly hard. The tines of her fork made a horrid scraping sound on her plate, and her cheeks flushed in embarrassment. She chewed the offending vegetable slowly and thoroughly before attempting to continue any sort of conversation.

Carrot conquered, and embarrassment partially faded, she made a second attempt at small talk. "I would tell you about my uncles, but I believe you already know how they do. Well," she said with a wave of her hand in Darcy's direction and a glance toward Rycroft, "at least the ones who remain."

Her cheeks flushed again. She had not meant for the comment to sound as unfeeling as it did. "I mean to say we have had a great deal of loss in our family over the past six years. Rycroft's father, Darcy's, my own." She hated how her voice always caught whenever she mentioned her father's death. It had been nearly six years. When would it ever become a topic about which she could speak without that feeling of despair gripping her heart as it did?

"I was sorry to hear of your father's passing," Alex said softly.

"Thank you," she whispered and bowed her head so that she could not see the understanding in his eyes. Of course, he knew how dearly she had loved her father, for she had spoken of it to him on more than one occasion.

As Alex watched her fidget with the napkin in her lap and draw several silent deep breaths, he began to reason out her refusal just a bit as a particular conversation came to mind. It was a conversation that had caused her to act then as she was now.

<hr />

"He wanted to take me to Bath to see the assembly rooms, and I wished for him to take the waters, but my mother will not allow it," she had fumed as they rode the length of a long field near Rosings.

The comment had shocked him. Anne's father had been ill for several months – three, at least. It had not appeared to be anything grave or oversetting but rather a general attitude of malaise.

"Why?" he had asked.

"My uncle requires assistance, and so the money that father had set aside for our journey had to be given to Lord Matlock."

She had fidgeted with the reins in her hands and drawn several deep breaths as quietly as she was now. Then, she had continued.

"Lord Matlock must not be refused. He is an earl after all, and my father is merely a baronet. The will of one comes before and at the expense of the other." She shrugged. "It is just the way things are and always will be."

She had then clucked to her horse and galloped ahead of him, and the topic was at an end. She would not return to it, no matter how many times and in how many ways he had attempted to broach it again.

Alex leaned close to his friend and whispered. "I had not considered, when playing, how a pawn might feel being used at the expense of the more powerful pieces on the board."

Jonathan's brows furrowed.

Alex tipped his head toward Anne, just slightly – not enough to draw anyone's attention but enough to direct his friend's thoughts.

"I was just thinking about how you accused me of protecting my knight above all," he explained, "and I began to consider how the other pieces might view such treatment. The pawns would think nothing of it as that is the way of rank." He shrugged. "Perhaps I might win more games if I treated the pawns as carefully as I did the pieces of rank such as the knight."

Jonathan's brows remained furrowed.

"It is as you said. There is often a reason for every action." He smiled at his friend's continued look of confusion. "I am sure you will see what I mean eventually," he concluded and turned back to his meal.

"Do you play chess?" Anne asked.

Alex nodded. "I do. I do not play well, but I do play. Do you?"

"On occasion."

"My brother is quite good," Miss Darcy interjected. "I have beaten him once, but I think he allowed it." She giggled and leaned forward as she whispered, "Elizabeth is helping me learn, so that he will not need to allow me to win next time."

"And is Mrs. Darcy a good player?" Jonathan asked.

Georgiana smirked. "My brother does much more huffing and shushing when he plays her than when he plays me."

Her three companions chuckled at this.

"I have often thought that the pawns were the bravest," she added. "They march forward into battle with little power to protect themselves, but always with the intent of protecting their king." She shrugged. "I find that brave."

"I had not considered it as such," said Jonathan, "but I would have to agree."

"I would not choose to be a pawn, however," Georgiana replied with a smile. "I am not so very brave."

"And what piece would you be?" Alex asked.

Georgiana pursed her lips and furrowed her brow. "I had not considered it."

"I would be the queen," Anne answered. "She can move as she wants and holds great power. The others will often protect not only the king but the queen as well, and," she lifted her fork as she made her point, "a pawn will march his way across a board, facing danger at every move, just to become a queen."

"I would not like to be the queen," Miss Darcy said softly. "I would not wish such a great responsibility."

"Responsibility? What responsibility?" Anne asked.

"Oh, I believe she has the most responsibility of all the pieces," Miss Darcy declared. "If she is captured, does she not put every other piece in greater danger, including the king?" She blushed. "I like to imagine the king and queen love each other." She made the admission quietly. "I would hate to place any whom I love in danger."

She was quiet for a moment, and her companions waited for her to continue, for she did look as if she had more to say.

"I have changed my mind," she finally said, "I think I would like to be a pawn, bravely defending those she loves – if only I could be so brave."

Alex nodded thoughtfully. He admired Miss Darcy's caring heart that would put herself in a place she did not wish to be to spare another from harm.

"I would still be the knight." He smiled. "Not only would I then get to defend my king and queen with my life, but I would also get to ride a horse while doing so."

His tone may have been light, nearly a laugh, but the intensity with which he looked at Anne was far from light. Silently, he begged her to understand that he knew she longed to be protected and that he was offering himself in her service.

For a moment, she chuckled uneasily while the others laughed with ease, but then, she stopped on a gasp as her eyes met his. Had she understood him? Or was it something else? He opened his mouth to ask her if she was well. However, he never spoke, for as Anne held his gaze, her eyes began to shimmer with unshed tears. His heart broke at the sight of it and continued to crumble as she sadly shook her head, rejecting his offer, before pushing her chair back, rising quickly, and hurrying from the room.

Chapter 17

ANNE FOUND A CORNER in the library and curled into the lonely chair that sat there. The realization that what she had sought for years lay within her reach, if she were not too fearful to grasp, it washed over her and ran down her cheeks in the form of hot tears.

He would love her. He would fight for her. She had seen it in his eyes. If she were honest with herself, which seemed to be what her mind desired to be at this moment, she had known it when he had found her on the balcony not far from this room during the ball. And then, she had been reassured of the fact when he sat on the steps at Matlock House, insisting that he be allowed to see her. Yet, he did not force her into any decision. He did not take from her the right to decide as others had tried to do.

She refused to think further and gave herself over to her tears until sometime later, when a hand gently shook her shoulder. She opened her eyes to find Elizabeth standing next to her.

"Is the chair large enough for two?" Elizabeth asked.

Anne dried her eyes as she straightened and slid over to the left, leaving just enough room for Elizabeth to squeeze in next to her. It was a cozy fit, but not uncomfortable. In fact, it felt quite welcoming to be so snugly situated.

This was one of the things she had enjoyed about getting to know her new cousins and their sisters. There was always an arm to be held, a hug to be given, or a smile to be shared. They were things she had not experienced before and had come to enjoy quite thoroughly.

"This is like when I sit with my sisters sometimes," Elizabeth commented. "Chats, when tucked in so closely, are really the best sort."

She placed a hand on top of Anne's and gave her a questioning look, waiting for a small nod of Anne's head before wrapping her hand around Anne's.

"You are distraught, and I am here to listen. A lady must not bear all her own burdens, or she becomes easily overwhelmed." She paused and leaned just a little closer to Anne as she whispered, "You may tell me yours. I promise I am very good at keeping secrets. Is it Mr. Madoch?"

Anne sighed and nodded but was unable to put her jumbled thoughts into words.

"May I tell you a secret?" Elizabeth smiled at Anne. "I am expecting a child. I have told few about it — only Mary, Kitty, Jane, and now you."

"Not Darcy?" Anne asked in surprise. She was to be told something before Elizabeth told her husband?

Elizabeth shook her head.

A small smile touched Ann's lips. She had been included in a secret with Elizabeth's sisters.

"I will tell Fitzwilliam soon. Perhaps after Kitty's wedding. I do not wish to detract from her day." She shifted a bit in the chair. "I suppose I will not be able to sit so snuggly for much longer."

Anne laughed lightly and agreed.

"I must tell you something else that only a few know." She laughed. "Actually, it was Mary who made me realize it. She is quite wise.

"You see, I became betrothed to my husband against my wishes. I thought him proud and unfeeling. I had heard him say something unflattering about me and allowed it to injure my pride, and when a lady's pride is injured, she is not always wise in her actions, and I was not wise. I listened to gossip about him and looked for things to criticize.

"I begged my father not to force me to accept him. I was certain that my life was doomed to be unhappy. But, I was wrong; very, very wrong. I soon learned that the man I was bound to was not at all the one whom I thought him to be, and though I was loath to admit it, I soon grew to love him."

She sat a bit straighter in the chair and cleared her throat with a little cough. "I am going to ask you some questions that Mary asked me. I do not know your heart or the full story of your acquaintance with Mr. Madoch, but they may help you just the same. You need not speak; a simple nod will suffice."

Anne nodded, and Elizabeth began.

"Is Mr. Madoch an honourable man?"

Anne thought of her interactions with him in the past and the night he had rescued her from Mr. Blackmoore on the balcony and nodded. He was honourable. Very much so.

"Is he solicitous of your feelings?"

Anne nodded quickly. She did not have to contemplate that. He had always – from their first meeting – been considerate of how she felt.

"And he cares for you, does he not?"

Again, Anne nodded. He had said he did six years ago, and even a lady as foolish and stubborn as she was at times could not deny that a man who was willing to face rejection over and over again and yet not force his desires onto her own had to love her.

"Do you fear he will ever treat you ill?"

That was the question, was it not? It was the one thing that had kept her from following where her heart led for the past six years. Anne cocked her head to the side and shook it slowly. "I very much think he is incapable of doing so," she admitted.

Elizabeth lowered her voice. "This is the most important question. Will you be content to be parted from him and given to another?"

Fresh tears sprang to Anne's eyes at the thought. She shook her head. "But he is of little standing," she protested weakly.

Elizabeth wrapped her arms around Anne. "Standing has almost nothing to do with happiness or love," she said softly. She squeezed Anne just a bit more tightly before releasing her and adding, "You must examine your heart and do what it says." She wiggled her way out of the chair. "The gentlemen will be joining us soon in the drawing room. I should be there so that Darcy does not worry." She looked down at Anne. "Will you join us?"

Anne nodded. "In a moment."

"Good, for if you do not, several others will come looking for you."

Anne smiled as Elizabeth left the room. It was comforting to know that there were others who cared about her wellbeing. She stood and walked to the terrace door. It was a cool evening but not too cold, so she pushed the door open and stepped outside. A bit of fresh air might help dry her tears and freshen her face.

"Miss de Bourgh?"

She looked down at the gentleman standing in the garden. "Mr. Blackmoore. Why are you not with the other gentlemen?"

"And why are you not with the other ladies?" he replied.

"I needed some air."

"So did I." He came to stand just below where she was. "I wish to apologize," he said. "I behaved poorly the last time we met."

A snort of laughter escaped Anne. "I should say you did." She tilted her head to the side and raised a brow. "Do you wish for me to believe you are reformed?"

He shook his head. "I am not sure I am reformed, but I am betrothed. It seems it is rather difficult to earn the trust of a lady or her relations when one has acted inappropriately and had his friendship with someone like Rycroft severed or nearly so. Therefore, while you may not believe this, I have decided to take my betrothal with some seriousness. Miss Bingley seems to be my only hope for pleasing my father."

"Is that so?" Anne snorted in laughter again as he chuckled somewhat bitterly.

"Indeed, it is. I have tried calling on others of greater standing, but alas, none seem willing to be home to me."

That seemed proper. In Anne's way of thinking, he was not the sort of gentleman any young lady of value should entertain as a suitor.

"Have you dismissed your mistress?"

He gave one sharp nod. "For now, at least. Whether it stays that way or not has yet to be seen."

Anne shook her head and rolled her eyes. At least, he would not be her problem. "How considerate of you," she said dryly.

He shrugged. "I did say that I might not be reformed."

"In case you were wondering, I will not marry a man with a mistress, nor will I become one." She thought it only wise to make sure he understood her position on such things completely since he did seem to lack a bit of sense about them.

Blackmoore laughed. "I would not even attempt to suggest such a thing. I felt the way Madoch protected you the last time we met, and I have endured his glares all evening." He shook his head as he continued to chuckle. "No, no, he is not someone with whom I wish to tangle. I fear I would not win."

The comment surprised Anne. "I beg your pardon, but I do not understand your meaning. What exactly makes a man who cares for horses someone who must be feared?" Alex was not a small or retiring man, but he was not a brute either. How he could inspire such a reaction in a gentleman who was his superior in rank was beyond her comprehension.

Blackmoore laughed once again. "His connections, my dear, his connections. It is not that he cares for horses but for whose horses he cares."

"His uncle?" The question leapt from her lips and with a tone that spoke of her utter disbelief.

Blackmoore shook his head. "Not unless his uncle is heir to the throne." He gave her a slight bow and walked off toward another open door.

Anne's mouth hung open for some minutes. "No, surely not," she said as she turned toward the open door of the library. "No, he could not be responsible for those horses." She closed the door behind her.

Chapter 18

"Are you well?"

Anne jumped at the sound of Rycroft's voice as it snatched her from her contemplation of what Mr. Black-moore had just told her.

"I may not be now," she scolded as he apologized for having startled her.

"Mr. Madoch has left." Rycroft extended his arm to her. "The drawing room should be safe."

Her heart jumped to a gallop. Alex was gone? "Why did he leave? You did not toss him out, did you?"

"You were speaking to him and then became distraught. What did you think I would do?"

Anne gasped in horror. "Oh, no, he did nothing to upset me. My distress was of my own creation. I have had a rather trying day." She shook her head and gripped his arm tightly. "You must go fetch him back. Oh, I feel dreadful." She held a hand to her forehead.

"I did not send him packing," Rycroft admitted.

"Then why did you say you did?" Anne pulled her arm away from him. "Oh, you are so vexing!" She stamped her foot.

Rycroft smiled. "He left of his own accord – he received a summons or some such thing."

"A summons? What has happened?"

Rycroft sighed. "I knew I would not be good at this, but Mary insisted I speak to you. It seems a horse was injured earlier today, and his expertise was needed. I do not know why it must be him, but then why does Prinny do half the things he does?" Rycroft's eyes grew large, and he clapped his mouth shut quickly.

"So, it is true? He tends to the royal horses?"

Rycroft nodded. "I was not to tell you."

"You did not. Mr. Blackmoore did." She turned toward the terrace door. "Just now, before you startled me, I was speaking to him in the garden." She spun back toward her cousin. "Why was I not to know? Why would he not tell me?"

Rycroft sighed once more. "He did not wish for you to choose him for his position or his wealth, about which I am also not supposed to tell you. However, I will say that it is not an insignificant figure."

Anne blinked, and her mouth dropped open slightly. How much had Alex hidden from her?

"Look." Rycroft took her arm and led her to a chair. "I am sure I will bungle this, but I will at least make an attempt to explain."

He let her take a seat and then paced before her. "When a man loves a woman, he will do nearly anything to secure his happiness, but he would not do it at the expense of hers. Any man of sense who wishes to have a marriage based on affection often waits to see if he has a chance of success – that the lady he loves might care for him – before he acts. Madoch is most certainly a man of sense.

Therefore, if Madoch had told you of his standing, you might have selected him based solely on that information, and he would never know if you cared for him or his position. And it is important to men such as Madoch that their wives prefer them above all else."

He sat on the edge of the seat across from her. "Do you understand?"

Anne nodded slowly. "I believe I do, but I have always loved him." And she was certain that Alex knew that.

Rycroft's took her hands. "But not enough," he said softly, "and that is what he wished to know – that you loved him enough to look past his position and accept him as a second son with a small inheritance and a love of horses. Do you understand?"

Anne nodded. Her stomach twisted again with regret – just as it had before she had left the dining room. And just as then, tears once again threatened to fall. It was not that she had not loved him enough, it was that she had allowed her fears to overwhelm that love. She had allowed her heart to be overruled by her head. It was not something she would do again. If only she could see him and tell him.

"Shall I call for the admiral's carriage?" Rycroft was looking at her in concern.

She nodded again. "Yes, please. I find I am not well after all."

Anne held the second of two returned letters in as many weeks. She tore open the seal to the letter that accompanied it and plopped into a chair. Her eyes scanned the brief contents of the missive. Alex was not in Brighton, according to his uncle.

She tossed the letters on the table and rested her head against the back of her chair, desperation began to worm its way up and around her heart. She had called at Lord Brownlow's the day after the dinner at Rycroft's. She had wanted to tell Alex of her change of heart, of her willingness to consider him no matter his circumstances, but he had been gone, without a word, save that he had business.

She sighed and rose to complete the few things she needed to do before she left Matlock House. Her cousin would marry the day after tomorrow, and then, she would return to Rosings and settle into life with her mother. She groaned at the thought. Perhaps she could visit her cousins frequently and avoid spending too much time with Lady Catherine.

Darcy would soon have a child. She could help care for the infant. Was that not what spinster relations did? Surely, Rycroft or Richard would add to the number of new family members soon. And perhaps, since Jane was so obliging, she might be willing to allow Anne to visit and tend to any Bingley offspring. She would hold that as a last hope, however. She had very little desire to spend any length of time with Miss Bingley or Lord Blackmoore.

She glanced at the clock. Half an hour. She had half an hour until she would conclude her one and only short season in town. It had not been completely without enjoyment. She had attended two balls, three musicales, and a dinner party. She had entertained several callers and taken in several of the sites of London.

She tucked a sketch into her book. It was a drawing given to her by Kitty and depicted one of the marbles at the museum. She had enjoyed seeing the lifelikeness of the stone. It still amazed her that so much life could come from something so hard and cold. She sniggered. The coldness of that trip had not been solely due to the stone facades of the marbles. No, Miss Bingley and her friends had been there.

"They like to frequent this display," Kitty had whispered, "but even the statues are unwilling to offer for the likes of them."

Both Anne and Kitty had laughed at the comment and returned to their drawing. Anne was not particularly good at drawing, but Kitty was willing to give her some instruction, and Anne was desirous of spending time with Kitty. They had ignored the other ladies after that. If only Miss Ivison had been so kind and reciprocated the action, but she was not. There was very little that was kind about Miss Ivison.

After making a round of the displays, Miss Ivison had come to admire the marble that Kitty and Anne were drawing. She stood off to the left, but not so far away that her conversation could not be heard by the two who were sketching.

"She has turned away an army of offers as if she is the prize of the season." Miss Pearce had tittered.

"And yet," Miss Ivison had continued, "she will return home in failure, an old maid. Fitting, I should think. Advertising for a husband," she scoffed. "No respectable woman does such a thing."

It had been enough to raise Anne's ire, and ignoring the restraining hand Kitty placed on her arm, she had stood and engaged the woman.

"And you do not advertise for a husband?" She looked at Miss Ivison's hat. "You could not make yourself more conspicuous than you do with that monstrosity on your head. It is like a beacon on the sea shouting to all who pass that danger lies just beyond it." Her gaze lowered. "And, if that neckline is not an advertisement as to what can be had... well." She had flicked an eyebrow and smirked. "Perhaps you should try an advertisement in the Times. I had several well-qualified gentlemen lining up to see me, and yet, even with what paltry goods you have to place on display..." She looked around the room and shook her head. "No one seems to be seeking you out."

She had then turned to Caroline. "I do not like you, but even you should know that this woman was keen to have me accept a most indecent proposal from Lord Blackmoore. And do you know why? Because she believes that a title should stay with those who are born to it rather than being given to those, such as yourself, who are of more lowly birth." She had paused. "You would do well to relieve yourself of such clawing females, but I suspect you are not so clever as to do so. Come, Kitty. I think there must be a more pleasant place to pass our time."

She still giggled at the look of displeasure on Miss Ivison's face. There had been a short conversation, conducted in harsh tones, as Kitty and Anne had walked away. Then, as they reached the door, Anne had looked back to see Miss Bingley and Miss Pearce arm in arm and Miss Ivison standing quite alone. She probably should have felt some pang of remorse or sadness for the lady, but she did not. She had felt rather elated, and she still did.

"Are you ready?" Lady Sophia poked her head around the door.

"Soon," Anne said. "If I could have five minutes, please. I need to do one more thing."

"Very well, but do hurry. Reginald grows restless. Military men do not like to be kept waiting."

Anne smiled at her aunt. It was true. The admiral was a stickler for punctuality, but he would have to wait just a moment. He would also have to adjust his route a small amount – that was also something of which a man like the admiral was not overly fond.

Be that as it may, there was something that really needed doing before she departed London, and to that end, she sat at the desk and opened her writing supplies. She dipped her pen in the ink and then, applying it to paper, began one last very important message.

"*It is with an anxious heart that I, Miss de Bourgh, once again apply to the readers of this paper...*"

Chapter 19

ALEX TOSSED HIS HAT and coat onto a chair near the table that had been set up for him in his room at the inn where he and Jonathan were staying. Another two days, and they would be back home at his estate where they would start arranging things how they needed to be to start breeding horses that others would travel for days to buy. Then, he'd be sitting at his own table rather than a small one in the corner of a rented room.

He sat down in the chair across from Jonathan and sighed. It had been a busy, but successful, day. Lord Brownlow now owned the hunters he desired, and in the process of advising Brownlow, Alex had come into possession of a fine mare to add to his own stables. She was just now getting settled in the inn's stables and waiting to be ridden home by one of his grooms tomorrow.

His business had gone well and promised to be even better in the future. He should be happy, but that was an emotion he doubted he would ever truly feel again. He had gambled his last chance at happiness two weeks ago with a foolish comment about chess. He closed his eyes and tried to block out the memory of Anne shaking her head with such sorrow in her eyes.

"Are the horses well?" Jonathan asked.

Alex nodded. "They are."

"And Brownlow is gone?"

Another nod. "He is, and he seems quite pleased."

"As he should be. That was a fine pair of horses he purchased."

"I would not have advised him to buy them if they were not – even if he did seem enamoured with them." Alex chuckled at how Brownlow had so easily taken to one of the horses in the pair when it had walked right up to him and poked at the pocket of his coat as if looking for some sort of treat.

Alex took up the piece of linen next to his place setting and placed it on his lap as he prepared to eat. The cook at this particular inn was well-known for his talent, and Alex was looking forward to enjoying it.

"There is a bit in here that you may wish to read." Jonathan folded the newspaper he had been reading so that only one small portion of a page was showing and placed it next to Alex's plate.

He pushed the paper away. "I will read it after I have had my fill."

He scooped a large spoonful of stew from his bowl. He did not wish to be bothered with any news that might spoil his pleasure in enjoying a good meal; still, he was curious about the nature of the article.

"Is it about politics?" he asked before indulging in that first bite of savoury goodness cradled in his spoon.

"No." Jonathan took a slow sip of his ale.

Madoch's brows furrowed as he chewed. "So, then, it is nothing to do with Prinny?" he questioned around the food in his mouth.

"No." Jonathan placed his mug on the table and leaned back in his chair. His plate was already empty because he had begun eating while Alex had stopped to question the stable boy about some item of care for his horses.

Madoch stretched his neck forward a bit as he took another bite. His eyes could just see a bit of the paper. If he had not pushed it so far, he might be able to read it as he ate.

"A society bit?" The words were nearly lost as they mixed with the stew in his mouth. Usually, his manners were better, but when it was just he and Jonathan, he often slipped into a more relaxed and far less formal habit than would be acceptable in polite society.

"You could say that," Jonathan said with a grin. "A wedding announcement might also be a fitting description depending on how *you*," he gave Alex a pointed look, "read it." He took up the paper. "I could read it to you if you wish."

Alex shrugged and broke off a piece of bread to sop up some of the liquid on his plate. "It matters not if I read it or if you do, I suppose."

"Does that mean I should read it?"

Alex nodded.

"You are certain?"

Alex scowled and nodded once again. Why would he not be certain he wished to hear a society announcement? He stopped eating as a reason registered in his mind, and the wonderful taste of stew in his mouth became sodden and dull. There was only one reason why Jonathan would think he did not wish to hear the announcement.

"Has she made a choice?"

Jonathan raised only one brow, and Alex knew that she had. He lowered his spoon, wiped his hands, and took a large gulp of his ale.

"Proceed," he said, steeling himself to hear the dreaded news that Anne would never be his.

"You will not believe her choice." Jonathan made a show of snapping the paper into position to read.

"Just get on with it."

"It is with an anxious heart that I, Miss de Bourgh, once again apply to the readers of this paper." Jonathan glanced up from the paper. "Are you sure you wish for me to continue?"

"Did I not say I did?" Alex barked. This was not like his friend. Jonathan did as instructed and rarely questioned more than once before proceeding.

"It is with an anxious heart that I, Miss de Bourgh, once again apply to the readers of this paper..." Again, Jonathan looked up from the words. "She would be gone to Hertfordshire by now for her cousin's wedding."

"I know," Alex said through clenched teeth.

Jonathan nodded and returned to the page. "It is with —"

Alex snatched the paper away from his friend. "You have read that bit twice already."

He took his time positioning the paper so that it could be easily read. Then, he blew out a great breath before turning his eyes to the words on the page and reading the few lines that were there. His brows furrowed, and he shook his head. Surely, he had not read that correctly. He began again. No. No, it seemed to say what he thought it did.

He handed the paper back to Jonathan. "It might be best if you read it. It seems my mind is playing tricks on me."

Jonathan took the paper from him. "It says exactly what you think, my friend, but I shall read it, without further delay, just to prove to you that it is true."

He cleared his throat and began reading. "It is with an anxious heart that I, Miss de Bourgh, once again apply to the readers of this paper for help in the search for a husband. As you, the reader, may know, I advertised not a month ago for a husband. I have made my selection; however, I fear I have taken too long in reaching my decision, and this gentleman may indeed be lost to me. And so it is with a trembling hand that I place this announcement here for all to see in hopes that one Mr. Alexander Madoch will be among the readers of this fine paper." Jonathan lowered the paper. "We can stay with my father," he said quietly.

Alex stared blankly at his friend for a moment. "She chose me," he said at last, "but why?" He rubbed his neck. "Do you suppose it is because she found out that I cared for the prince's horses?" Brownlow had shared that bit of news with him. Apparently, Blackmoore had told Anne about the connection.

"Ask her."

"Ask her?" That did seem to be the logical thing to do but how? She was in Hertfordshire, and he was not.

Jonathan chuckled softly. "Yes, my friend. Ask her. We leave at first light and will stay with my father. I shall inform the stables and innkeeper of the change." He had risen and was standing at the door before he had finished speaking. "I know I did not approve of her when we started this scheme of yours. However, I have changed my position on the matter and will not allow you to refuse her for any reason." And without waiting for any sort of reply from Alex, he quit the room.

Alex once again applied himself to his meal, which had, remarkably, grown tastier in the time it had sat untended. As he scooped a final spoonful of stew from his plate, he exhaled deeply. His days of eating alone or with only Jonathan were at an end. Finally. Finally. His happiness was within his reach, and as soon as he reached Hertfordshire, he would grasp it and never let go.

He looked at his watch and considered running after his friend to inform him that they would be leaving now. However, the day was growing late, and while he knew the likelihood of his sleeping at all tonight was limited, the horses needed their rest. Perhaps it was best if they left in the morning. It had been a long day, after all, but...

He shook his head. No. They would leave tomorrow. He had waited for Anne for six years already. He was nearly certain he could wait just a little longer. Most likely.

Chapter 20

IT HAD BEEN A long day even though it had only really just begun. Anne had smiled when she was supposed to and had attempted to say all the right things, but her heart, though happy for her cousin and Kitty, was anything but joyous.

It had been two days since she had placed that advertisement in the paper, and she could not help wondering if Alex had seen it and whether the joy she had seen on Kitty's face today would ever be hers.

"You look tired." Lady Sophia came to stand near her in Netherfield's drawing room.

Anne gave a small shrug. "I am, I suppose."

"A bit of air might help. Will you take a walk with me?" Lady Sophia sent a footman scurrying with the request for both her wrap and Anne's as soon as Anne had agreed to take a walk. "It was a lovely wedding breakfast, was it not?"

Anne nodded. "It was beautiful."

"I only have two nieces left to see happy." The look she gave Anne was gentle. "I will see them both happy, will I not?"

Anne shook her head. "I cannot say," she whispered. She pulled her lips into a smile that she did not feel. "However,

I will attempt to be happy. If I can spend time with you and my cousins and their wives, I think I can be at least content." She shook her head again. "If I have to spend all my time with my mother, I will be neither content nor happy — although perhaps I will learn to enjoy her company."

"Am I to understand, then, that you will not marry anyone but Mr. Madoch?" It was the third time since entering the carriage yesterday that her aunt had asked that question.

"I will not." Anne took her wrap from her maid and, putting it on, followed her aunt into the garden. It was a bright, crisp day, and the freshness of the air felt good as she drew a deep breath.

"Not even for security or position?" Lady Sophia wound her arm around Anne's and pulled her close as they walked to a bench surrounded by some early blooms and protected by a hedge.

"If I found myself destitute, I might," Anne replied, "but I do not see that happening. I have you, Uncle Reginald, and my cousins, who I know would come to my aid."

Lady Sophia patted Anne's hand. "That we would. But, I must say, this is a great change for you, is it not – to be dependent on others and under their power?"

"None of you would ever harm me." Anne took a seat on the bench. "You love me far too much to allow it."

Lady Sophia smiled but did not sit next to Anne. "We do, and I am glad you have come to realize it."

She turned to look down the path. "Your father loved your mother, you know." She spoke quietly, glancing back at Anne. "He applied to my father three times before his offer was accepted." Her shoulders rose and fell with a great breath. "But there were stipulations placed on the agreement. My brother, your uncle, the current Lord Matlock, was not the best at balancing wants with income. He has since improved, but I would still not trust him with my money."

She took a seat next to Anne. "It is not his strength. My father knew this and used the love your father had for my sister to coerce an agreement of support, should it become necessary, which we all knew was an inevitable event, and you know, of course, how important appearance is to your mother. I can only imagine the begging and threatening that might have taken place if your father had not wished to give my brother what he requested." She took Anne's hand. "My imagination is not wrong in this, is it?"

"No, you are not wrong. There were many loud discussions." Her reply was soft, and Lady Sophia had to bend closer to hear it.

"I am sorry to hear that."

There was a question that had always tugged at Anne's mind and knowing her aunt as well as she did now, she dared to ask it. "Did my mother ever love my father?"

"I do not know, my dear. I certainly never saw it. There was admiration and concern, but nothing of the giving of one's very soul to the other, as I had with my husband." She sighed. "That is where the issue lay – not with rank or fortune, but with a lack of the best kind of love. But I think you understand that now."

"I do," Anne admitted softly. It was just too bad that understanding that fact had come too late.

"I always have."

Anne gasped as Alex stepped around the hedge, and her lips trembled while tears sprang to her eyes at the sight of him.

"A man or woman who loves another completely would not allow harm to come to the one they love, no matter the source."

"It is good to see you, Mr. Madoch," Lady Sophia said as she stood and offered her place next to Anne.

"Be happy," she whispered as she gave Anne's cheek a kiss. And then, she was gone.

"You came," Anne whispered as Alex sat down beside her and took her hand. "I was afraid you would not. I called on you at Lord Brownlow's, and I made my uncle give me the directions for a letter to you."

"You wrote to me?"

Anne nodded and lifted her gaze from their joined hands to his eyes. "Twice. The second letter was returned with an accompanying letter from your uncle explaining that you were not in Brighton and would not be for some time." She bit her lip to keep it from trembling and drew a shuddering breath. "I thought I had lost you. Why did you leave?"

"I had some business to which to attend, and I thought I had bungled my last chance with you." He lifted one hand to her face and stroked her cheek. It was the most comforting thing she had ever felt, for in his gentle touch she could feel his care for her. "Why did you choose me?" he asked.

"I love you," she said without a moment's pause. "I have always loved you."

"Then it was not because of what Mr. Blackmoore told you about my connections?"

Anne's eyes grew wide, and she shook her head vigorously. "I had made my choice before I knew. What he or Rycroft may have told me afterward were of little concern."

"Rycroft?"

"My cousin sought me out after I left the dining room to see if I was well, and he accidentally confirmed what Mr. Blackmoore had said."

Alex tilted his head and studied her face. "I am no longer in charge of the Prince's stables in Brighton."

She blinked. That seemed a sudden change of circumstances. Not that it changed how she felt about him at all. She smiled as she realized with even more certainty than she already held that what he was in the eyes of society could not and would not change how her heart belonged to him. "Have you been sacked? Was the prince angry that you left town so suddenly?"

He chuckled. "No, I, or rather Jonathan, made arrangements for me to step down from my position."

Lightness bubbled up in her heart and tipped her lips into a teasing smile. "So, you will not be sent to the tower or off to some foreign land?"

He pulled her into his embrace. "I will be contentedly managing my own stables on my own estate and providing guidance as needed in Brighton as well as a well-bred horse to the Brighton stables on occasion."

"May I join you?" She looked up at him from where her head rested a bit awkwardly on his shoulder. "Will you have me?"

"You truly do not care that my position has changed and that I might fade completely from Prinny's notice?"

"Not even a little bit." She smiled sheepishly at him. "I have been a fool."

His left brow rose, and he smirked. "I will not disagree. You have been, and I am sure you will continue to be at times."

With a huff, she tried to pull away from him, but he was not letting go.

"Be that as it may," he continued, giving her that smile that made her stomach flip, "you will be my fool, and I will be glad to have you." He released her suddenly and stood, leaving her quite confused. "Come," he said extending his hand. "We have a journey to make."

"A journey?" She placed her hand in his.

"Yes," he said with a smile, "a journey."

"To where?" she asked as he pulled her to her feet and back into his embrace.

"Do you trust me?"

"Completely."

"Good," he said before giving her a most delightful kiss.

"I have waited six years to have you as my wife," he said after he had broken the kiss and held her tightly as his chest rose and fell rapidly at first but then slowed to something closer to normal well before Anne's did.

"I will not wait another moment longer than I must," he continued, and then bending, he scooped her into his arms and hurried through the garden and to the carriage – Rycroft's carriage – that stood waiting on Netherfield's drive.

"What are you doing?" Anne demanded as Alex deposited her inside Rycroft's travelling coach.

"Did I not tell you that we have a journey to go on?" He winked at her as he climbed in and took the seat next to her.

"To where?"

"To Scotland, of course," he said as the door to the carriage closed.

"We are going to Scotland?" Anne was positive that she had heard him correctly, but still the thought was so shocking that it demanded confirmation.

"I will not wait three weeks for banns to be read." The carriage lurched forward. "Nor will I spare the time or expense for a license, so we will be married in Gretna Green by the end of the week." Alex pulled her back against him. "Your things are securely fastened to the roof, as are mine."

"And my maid?" Anne asked.

"Will not be needed." Alex tightened his grip on her so that she could not jump away from him.

"We are not married," she scolded as she settled back against his side after a brief struggle to free herself. To be quite honest, she was not entirely unhappy that her attempt at escape had been thwarted. She rather liked the feeling of being snuggled next to him.

"Ah, but we will be." He grunted slightly when her elbow jabbed him in the side. "Very well, a maid can be secured at each stop."

"And I shall have my own room?"

Alex sighed. "If you insist."

"It is only proper."

Alex laughed. "My dear, what precisely is proper about advertising for a husband, announcing your selection in the paper, and then marrying at Gretna Green?" He looked down at her upturned face and kissed her forehead. "However, if it is what you want, then you shall have it."

She smiled and snuggled just a bit closer to him. "How did you manage all this? The carriage, my things, everything."

He chuckled and the sound rumbled through her in a most wonderful way. "I did not manage any of it. It seems Lady Sophia and the admiral, along with Mr. Lester, have conspired to see us happy. As I understand it, in two days' time, all the papers in London, will carry an announcement of our happy union." He squeezed her close. "You are happy, are you not?"

She nodded. "Very. And you?"

"I am. Though I suspect neither your mother nor your uncle will be too pleased when they discover that announcement in the paper."

She tilted her face to look up at him and brought the hand which was not pinned against his side up to rest on his cheek.

"I love you. I always have, and I always will. But more than that, I know with all that I am that you love me and will always, always protect me. How can I not know that when you are willing to anger the likes of my mother and uncle and quite possibly have to bear their reproach for the rest of your life?"

"I would endure far worse for you." He leaned toward her as if to kiss her but stopped just short of her lips. "Tell me again why you chose me."

She smiled and shook her head. "I did not choose you. My heart did."

No answer could have satisfied him more. His quest to secure her love was complete and the challenge to keep it had begun. He kissed her gently and then, ignoring her protest, lifted her onto his lap and kissed her more fully. As she wrapped her arms around his neck and ran her fingers through the hair that curled above his collar and as the carriage bounced and swayed on its journey, he knew that, no matter the trials that lay ahead, no matter the disagreements that were sure to arise, he could and would find solace in the knowledge that he was and always would be her heart's choice.

Epilogue

Dear Reader,

Happiness is not guaranteed. Indeed, it can be a right fickle emotion. One might find happiness only to have it removed, or one might find contentment which grows into a happiness of incomprehensible measure. It might elude the most deserving, or it might grace one who ill deserves it. Just as it might wax and wane in life, so too it may shift in the land of stories, guided, of course, by the pen of an author who, though following closely the personality of her characters, grants or refuses happiness to one and all.

The happiness or unhappiness of our players has developed in the following fashion:

We shall, of course, begin with the least deserving. Miss Ivison, as she is still called these five years after the close of our story, was never fortunate enough to find a gentleman willing to accept her – despite her fifteen thousand. However, that does not mean she went without notice to those seeking a lady willing to press the edges of propriety in an attempt to lure a partner. And so, she lives in a small house near her father's estate with few friends and a daughter, who will never be fully accepted into polite society, no matter the fact that her father held a title – even if he was only a Sir and not a Lord.

Ah, it is a sad tale for the young child to be sure, for her mother was to wed the man until, at about the same time that his penchant for cheating while playing cards with His Highness was discovered, his love of life began to outweigh his love of her dowry, and he skulked off one night to begin a life of travel. What became of him, no one truly knows, though small stories have occasionally surfaced now and again. None of these stories were flattering, however, but such is the life of a scoundrel.

Miss Pearce fared much better after the day she walked away from Miss Ivison in the museum. She found a pleasant gentleman with whom she could live comfortably and grew to love him dearly.

Miss Bingley was fortunate indeed. She has one son approaching his first birthday and another child to arrive in the summer, as well as a husband who keeps himself occupied with his estate when needed and escorts her to social events throughout the season.

She would tell you her life is perfect, but it's not. Having had her faith in friends severely shaken by Miss Ivison, she has few that she has allowed to become close, and so, she finds herself on occasion feeling quite lonely. Her husband has been a source of good fortune, for though he married her to gain his father's approval, he has come to care for her, and despite everyone's expectations that he would once again take up with a mistress, he has not. Whether that is due to his care for his wife and children or a fear of reprisals from his father or Mr. Bingley and his group of powerful friends and relations, it is hard to say, but no matter the reason, he has remained faithful.

Lord Brownlow has yet to choose a bride and fulfill his duty to his title, but a lovely lady from Hertfordshire, herself rather advanced in her years, has caught his eye. Should he not declare himself soon, Mrs. Darcy, the lady's particular friend, along with her husband and his cousin, Lord Rycroft, has planned a soiree for Charlotte's birthday at the end of the month, and her father has agreed to aid in whatever scheme they might employ to speed the happy conclusion of marriage between the two.

Mr. Collins, who was thwarted in his attempt to mend bridges through marrying a cousin, has found himself in possession of his inheritance while Mr. Bennet yet lives. He has taken up residence at Longbourn where he finds himself called on regularly by Mrs. Long and her nieces, as well as Mrs. King and her daughter, Miss Mary King, who was returned to Hertfordshire not long after the departure of the militia.

However, unless one mother or the other soon makes mention of their purpose in calling, it may be quite some time before Mr. Collins comes to the conclusion himself, and the entail upon Longbourn might indeed be in danger of dying with him.

Mr. Bennet, though he still lives under a heavy shadow of ill health, has, at the insistence of his daughters and sons, taken up residence in Bath. Since arriving in his handsome new home, with much complaining, he has found the waters to be to his liking nearly as much as the library which Mr. and Mrs. Darcy had fitted and filled for him.

Mrs. Bennet has discovered that Bath is near perfection for entertaining and being entertained, and, much to her husband's delight, spends a good deal of time in the company of new friends – and not in his library. The grandeur of their new home plays significantly on her happiness.

"It is like a dream," she often comments. "It is so large that we have to close off a floor when we are by ourselves. We quite rattle around in all that space when we do not have visitors." And then she smiles and adds, "My sons are quite wealthy you know, and such dears to see to our care as they have."

But do not fret; the Bennets are rarely lonely or given a lengthy period of time in which to rattle around. For at least twice a year, each of their daughters, with family in tow, come for a visit. And on many occasions, there is more than just one daughter in residence, as is the case at present.

This May, the Bennets' home is filled to capacity as sisters and cousins and children and aunts and uncles and friends have gathered to celebrate both the birthday of the man to whom so many of them owe their happiness and the marriage of the last Bennet daughter.

⁓ ⚮ ⁓

"This is quite the happy assembly, is it not?" Sir William asked as he settled into a chair near Mr. Bennet at the far end of the drawing room.

"That it is," Mr. Bennet agreed.

"Papa!" A dark-haired child with a rather serious look on his face and a tear on his cheek darted across to the room to Darcy. In one hand he held a book and in the other a page of that book. "Cousin Elinor ruined my book."

Darcy sighed and scooped his son onto his lap as Anne bit back a giggle and Alex, with a shake of his head, rose to go find his daughter, who was altogether too much like her mother.

"It was not nice," Darcy agreed with his son in an attempt to stop a protracted lecture by the boy from beginning in earnest. "One must treat books with care. However, we must also learn to forgive those who treat us ill."

Lucas scrunched up his face into a scowl, his lower lip protruding in displeasure. "She ruined my book," he grumbled.

"I take it you did not forgive her?" his father said.

Lucas shook his head.

"He pulled her hair," Michael, the eldest of Rycroft's three boys, supplied. "And then she threw a block at Amelia and hit her right on her head." He pointed to the right side of his head above his ear where the second youngest of the Bingley girls had been hit. "Amelia cried, of course." He rolled his eyes. "And then Elinor's papa came, but she is hiding." He smiled. "He'll not find her." There was a hint of pride in his voice. "Frederick helped her hide, and he is almost as good as me at hiding."

Rycroft snapped his fingers and motioned for Michael to come stand before him. "Where has your brother hidden your cousin?"

Michael's shoulders lifted and fell. "I do not know. They ran out of the nursery, and I did not follow them. I followed Lucas."

"You are certain you do not know?"

Michael shook his head, causing his sandy-coloured curls to bounce.

"Were there any other mishaps of which we," he motioned around the group of adults, "should know?"

Michael tilted his head to the side and thought for a moment. "The babies are sleeping," he said holding up three fingers to indicate his youngest brother, the Bingleys' youngest daughter, and Kitty's youngest son.

"The girls are drawing flowers." Three more fingers popped up. One for Lucas' sister and the other two for the remaining Bingley children. "And Theodore is building a castle with blocks, although he is rather angry at Elinor for interfering with his plans. I think he might send her to the tower."

Richard sighed. "You will tell me if he does send her to the tower, will you not, so that I can free her?"

Michael smiled and bobbed his head up and down.

"Immediately," Rycroft said.

The smile faded from his son's face. "Must I?"

"Yes. Will you?"

The lad's shoulders slumped dejectedly. "Yes."

"Very well, then, you are dismissed, young man." Rycroft scruffed up the child's hair and winked at him. "You have done your mother proud with your tale bearing."

Lady Rycroft coughed softly.

Her husband merely smiled at her.

The admiral, who was also seated with Mr. Bennet and Sir William, chuckled. "They are a lively lot, but I would expect no less, considering their parents."

"Indeed," Mr. Bennet agreed. "Despite their quirks, they are all quite perfect."

"No truer words have been spoken," the admiral said. "And I am sure that the Lesters and Endicotts will be adding to the number in due time."

"The gentlemen arrive tomorrow, and my wife is beside herself with excitement," Mr. Bennet said. "The other wedding breakfasts were all at Netherfield, so this is the first she will have the pleasure of hosting in our home." He shook his head. "Add to that the fact that Lydia is sharing her day with Georgiana, and you can imagine the delight which has effused from her on a daily basis for the past month and a fortnight."

Sir William chuckled.

"I am not truly complaining, for it is well within her rights to be excited as her final daughter will be happily situated," Mr. Bennet added with a smile. He could not fault his wife for her excitement, since he shared it with her. Each of his daughters would be married and happily so. Not one had married for convenience. They had each found a love match of good character and financial standing.

"My sister is just as delighted to see her last niece happy," added the admiral. "I had feared it would not happen, but it has, thanks to Darcy."

⌒﹏❦﹏⌒

It had been a long two seasons for Georgiana. She had found her heart quite gone before the first had even begun. A gentleman had unwittingly captured her fancy at a brief meeting over a meal at Rycroft Place five years ago, but not being out, she pined secretly for him until just before her debut when she spoke of it to her aunt.

From there, strategies were made, house parties planned, soirees attended, all with the intent of securing her happiness with the gentleman. It was not easily done, however, as the gentleman attended social events only sporadically.

Finally, after Georgiana had refused the fifth offer of marriage from as many eligible gentlemen, Darcy was made aware of the desires his sister's heart. A rather direct letter to the gentleman later, and Mr. Lester appeared at Darcy House to court the young lady whom he had found fascinating but feared was too far above him.

Lydia's story had been less filled with longing. She had happily made her debut next to Georgiana under the watchful eye of Mrs. Darcy and Mrs. Bingley and had been called on by several gentlemen, yet none truly captured her heart. She spoke of it often to a particular gentleman with whom she often found herself thrown together since he was Rycroft's friend. And he, in turn, spoke to her of his reluctance to marry for anything less than the deepest of affection. Their friendship grew and then quite unexpectedly shifted to something more, and now, Lydia found herself betrothed to her friend, the one man at whom she never batted an eyelash and with whom she had never acted a part.

So it was that a week later, both young ladies stood in this very drawing room, repeating their vows and tying their hearts forever to the men whom they loved, before sitting down to a sumptuous wedding breakfast.

❧

"I have a gift for my lovely bride." Jonathan rose as his announcement drew the attention of the rest of the wedding guests. He extended a hand to Georgiana and helped her to her feet. Then, he took a small pouch from his pocket and from it shook out a necklace.

"This is a symbol of love, both past and present – once for lovers long ago, and now for my love for you. As the pearl is locked away within this heart never to be removed, so your love is woven deeply into the fabric of my very being, never to be removed." He stepped behind her and fastened the necklace around her neck. "It belonged to my grandfather."

"It is lovely." Georgiana sighed as she held up the golden heart, woven in such a fashion as to look like it was a delicate cage for the pearl locked inside.

Mrs. Bennet's eyes grew wide at the sight of it. "It looks just like the one my father showed me," she whispered to Lady Lucas, who was on her left.

"It is the very same," Lady Lucas replied. "Mr. Lester's father came to work for Sir William's brother, and his father, Mr. Lester's grandfather, left that necklace as an inheritance to his son. It seems it has now been passed down to the grandson." She sighed. "And there is such a story behind it."

"Indeed, there is!" Mrs. Bennet smiled at her friend and grasped Lady Lucas' arm excitedly. "Passed down to the grandson, who has now given it to the granddaughter of Lady Matlock." She whispered but so excitedly that it was not as soft as it should have been. Thankfully, all who were gathered were family.

Lady Sophia nodded and smiled at Mrs. Bennet's comment. "Finally, the second necklace has come home," she said looking at her brother.

Several pairs of questioning eyes turned towards her as she dashed a tear from her cheek. "There is a story," she began. "It is a story of choices and unequal marriages and eventual happily ever afters." She held up a cautionary finger. "However, it must remain within our family..."

If you enjoyed this book, be sure to let others know by leaving a review.

~*~*~

Want to know when other Leenie books will be available?
You can always know what's new with my books by subscribing to my mailing list.

leeniebrown.com/subscribe

~*~*~

Turn the page to read an excerpt of another one of Leenie's books.

Two Days Before Christmas Excerpt

Now that you have come to the end of the Choices series, please, allow me to suggest my Darcy Family Holiday's series to you as a possible next read. This series starts with some scheming by Darcy's sister to give him the best Christmas present ever. Below is a portion of the first chapter of book 1, Two Days Before Christmas.

Georgiana Darcy peered out her bedroom window to see who had come to call and was causing the flurry of activity in the halls. Her eyes grew wide as she saw her brother step down from his travelling coach and give some directives to a footman — likely about his trunk or possibly requesting tea. Those were the things he most often thought of first when arriving home from a trip. Her brows furrowed, and her lips pinched into a displeased pucker. Her brother was not supposed to be here in town. He was supposed to be in Hertfordshire with Mr. Bingley, learning how to be something other than unpleasant.

Honestly! It was her heart that had been broken by that cad Wickham, not his! Hers was mending, but his? She shook her head. If only she could do something to prove to him that, though she had been hurt — and grievously so –, her heart was no longer affected. In fact, she had recently begun to think that it had never actually been touched at all. She had not been in love with Wickham. She was nearly convinced of that fact. She had been in love with the idea of being loved, adored, and cherished by a handsome man. That she had not been and feared she might never be was what still caused a pinching pain in her heart. Her companion, Mrs. Annesley, assured her it was a foolish notion to judge every gentleman by the actions of one, but it seemed prudent to Georgiana to be cautious, just in case. She had been too trusting. No one could tell her otherwise. However, just because she needed to learn a lesson in prudence, did not mean her brother needed to continue to suffer. He had done precisely as he should. Her pain was not his doing. The fact that he still tormented himself with guilt was what made it nearly impossible for her to lay her own, well-deserved, shame aside.

She had spoken in confidence about such things to Mr. Bingley before he and her brother had departed for Netherfield, Mr. Bingley's new estate. He had promised he would do his best to see her brother engaged in activities that would bring him distraction if not pleasure. She had been so hopeful that Mr. Bingley had been successful, for Fitzwilliam's letters had been light in tone, sharing stories of the various people he had met and wishing he was free of the attentions of one particular person, Caroline Bingley. Added to that, yesterday, Mr. Bingley had called to inform her that her brother had done the most unusual thing by dancing with a Miss Elizabeth — the same Miss Elizabeth that had featured in more than one of Fitzwilliam's missives.

Why he was home when things had seemed so promising, she was uncertain. She grabbed a wrap for her shoulders and slipped her feet into her slippers.

"Your brother has returned," Mrs. Annesley said as Georgiana met her in the corridor.

"I saw his carriage," Georgiana replied. "It is very unexpected."

"It is," Mrs. Annesley agreed. "Do you wish for me to attend you?"

Georgiana shook her head.

Mrs. Annesley glanced down the stairs. "You will tell me how he is, will you not?" There was a note of worry in her whispered question.

As far as Georgiana was concerned, hiring Mrs. Annesley to be her companion was the best gift Fitzwilliam had ever given her. Mrs. Annesley's heart was far softer than her angular features and austere manner of dress suggested. She was also aware of far more than the spectacles that perched on her nose while she read and stitched might indicate.

"Of course, I will," Georgiana assured her.

A twinkle shone in the lady's eye. "Then be quick."

Georgiana giggled as she descended the stairs. Mrs. Annesley was quiet and reserved, as was proper for one in her position, but she was also curious and lively when she and Georgiana were alone. Reaching the bottom of the stairs,

Georgiana stopped and waited patiently as her brother removed his outerwear and apologized to Mr. Wright, his butler, for the unexpected change in plans.

Seeing her, he greeted her first with a smile and then, open arms, which she ran into without a second's pause.

"I have missed you," he murmured against her hair before releasing her.

"You did not return on my account, did you?" Georgiana wrapped her arm around his.

"May I not wish to see my sister?"

His avoidance of her question was not a good sign. Such a tactic always meant he did not wish to discuss his reasons for something.

"You may wish to see her, but you should not do so at the expense of breaking your word to a friend." She felt his arm flinch. "Mr. Bingley called on me yesterday. He seemed eager to return to Hertfordshire." Again, his arm flinched.

"He may return anytime he wishes."

Her brows drew together. Her brother's tone was so flat, so uncaring — so very unlike him. "I assume Miss Bingley and the Hursts accompanied you back to town?"

"They did."

She lifted a brow and gave him an assessing look. "You know Mr. Bingley will never persuade Caroline away from town so close to the season. It was a struggle to get her to go with him at Michaelmas."

He shrugged? The only response she was going to receive to such a comment was a shrug?

"He will be disappointed," Georgiana said softly.

"That cannot be helped."

Georgiana's heart sank at Darcy's words. Mr. Bingley had been so eager to return to Netherfield and a particular lady. In fact, he had mentioned taking his mother's fede ring with him when he returned. Not returning would do more than disappoint Mr. Bingley; it would likely break his heart and the heart of the lady he had left behind.

"Now, as delighted as I am to see you," her brother continued, "I am desirous of a long soak in a hot tub of water." He gave her a tight smile. "To wash away the chatter of Miss Bingley."

He had not remembered to ask her if she was well. That was also odd. For the last several months, he had asked her that question at least three times a day and always upon returning from a time away. She released his arm but only to allow her hand to slide down and grasp his. "Fitzwilliam?" She waited until he looked up at her instead of at their joined hands before continuing. "Are you well?"

His eyes left hers and looked down the hall toward his room as he nodded. "I will be," he said as he lifted her hand and kissed her fingers. "I will be."

Georgiana pulled her lip between her teeth as she watched him walk down the hall to his room. His shoulders were not as square as they normally were, and he ran his hand through his hair which was something he only did when thoroughly overwhelmed by a situation. He was not well. Something was most certainly wrong.

Georgiana gasped as a reason for her brother's melancholy came to mind. Unwilling to entertain the troubling thought for hours before she spoke to her brother again, she hurried down the hall and knocked firmly on his door. Then she waited. There was some shuffling in the room, but none that sounded as if a person were approaching the door, so she knocked again. This time she rapt so loudly that she was positive at least one knuckle would bear a bruise from the action.

However, her sore knuckles had produced the desired effect since her brother, minus his coat and cravat, opened his door.

"She has not trapped you, has she?" Georgiana demanded.

Her brother's brows drew together in question. "I beg your pardon?"

"Caroline Bingley. She has not finally succeeded in trapping you into marriage while her brother was gone, has she?" Georgiana's heart raced with trepidation. Caroline Bingley was not the sort of lady she wished to have as a sister, nor did she think her brother would ever be happy married to such a person. Caroline was not horrid, but she was not gentle or lively or particularly witty. She was just not the sort of lady Georgiana knew her brother needed for a wife.

Thankfully, shock suffused her brother's face as he blurted an emphatic no.

"You are not marrying her?" Georgiana asked again just to be certain of his answer.

"No, Georgie, I am not marrying anyone." The light in his eyes faded as he said it.

In spite of her concern for the sadness in his tone and expression, Georgiana smiled at him. "One day you will," she said hopefully.

"Perhaps one day," he replied without so much as a hint of conviction that it was true.

Oh, he was in a deplorable state of mind, and Georgiana was quite certain she knew why.

"Was there anything else?" he asked as he turned to close his door.

Georgiana shook her head. "Not at the moment."

"Then, I shall see you at dinner."

Georgiana stared at his closed door. "Perhaps, nothing," she muttered. "You will marry one day, and you will be happy," she declared to the door, "even if I must see to it myself." Having settled the matter with her brother's closed door, she turned and went in search of Mrs. Annesley. Undoubtedly, her companion would have some advice as to how to help Fitzwilliam.

More Books by Leenie

You can find all of Leenie's books at this link

bit.ly/LeenieBBooks
where you can explore the collections below

❧

Dash of Darcy and Companions Collection

Marrying Elizabeth Series

Sweet Possibilities and Sweet Extras

Willow Hall Romances

The Choices Series

Darcy Family Holidays

Darcy and... An Austen-Inspired Collection

Teatime Tales (Sweet Austen-inspired Novelettes)

Other Pens

Touches of Austen

Nature's Fury and Delights (Sweet Regency Novelettes)

About Leenie

Leenie Brown has always been a girl with an active imagination, which, while growing up, was both an asset, providing many hours of fun as she played out stories, and a liability, when her older sister and aunt would tell her frightening tales. At one time, they had her convinced Dracula lived in the trunk at the end of the bed she slept in when visiting her grandparents!

Although it has been years since she cowered in her bed in her grandparents' basement, she still has an imagination which occasionally runs away with her, and she feeds it now as she did then — by reading!

Her heroes, when growing up, were authors, and the worlds they painted with words were (and still are) her favourite playgrounds! Now, as an adult, she spends much of her time in the Regency world, playing with the characters from her favourite Jane Austen novels and those of her own creation.

When she is not traipsing down a trail in an attempt to keep up with her imagination, Leenie resides in the beautiful province of Nova Scotia with her two sons and her very own Mr. Brown (a wonderful mix of all the best of Darcy, Bingley, and Edmund with a healthy dose of the teasing Mr. Tilney and just a dash of the scolding Mr. Knightley).

Connect with Leenie on her blog, social media, or in one of her subscription communities. Find links to all of those on her website at bit.ly/connect-with-leenie